# Breathless

J.M. LAMP

*This book is a work of fiction. Names, characters, businesses, organizations, places, events and incidents either are the product of the author's imagination or are used fictitiously. Any resemblance to actual persons, living or dead, events, or locales is entirely coincidental.*

*Book and Cover design by Joseph Lamp*
*ISBN: 9781521338759*
*First Edition: May 2017*
*10 9 8 7 6 5 4 3 2 1*

# Chapters:


CHAPTER ONE .......... 1
CHAPTER TWO .......... 16
CHAPTER THREE .......... 32
CHAPTER FOUR .......... 48
CHAPTER FIVE .......... 62
CHAPTER SIX .......... 76
CHAPTER SEVEN .......... 91
CHAPTER EIGHT .......... 102
CHAPTER NINE .......... 117
CHAPTER TEN .......... 132
CHAPTER ELEVEN .......... 150
CHAPTER TWELVE .......... 163
CHAPTER THIRTEEN .......... 177
CHAPTER FOURTEEN .......... 193
CHAPTER FIFTEEN .......... 205
CHAPTER SIXTEEN .......... 217
CHAPTER SEVENTEEN .......... 229
CHAPTER EIGHTEEN .......... 239
CHAPTER NINETEEN .......... 250
CHAPTER TWENTY .......... 262

*To everyone out*
*there who is still waiting for*
*their love story, it will be written eventually.*

# Chapter One

Elliot

WHEN YOU PLAY wingman for your best friend on a double date, and said friend only wants to have sex with the guy he is on the date with, the guy that ends up sitting across from you is always a real winner.

"Paul didn't tell me you were so damn cute, Elliot," Ricky says, twirling his straw around his lips. "I mean, honestly, you must really reel in the hotties." He throws his scarf over his right shoulder and tilts his head with a smile.

There are many types of gays in the world and Ricky is the exact opposite of what I'm attracted to. Ethan knows this.

"I do OK," I say, looking to the waitress bringing over our food. He leans his chin into his palm and expects more, I think, but he gets nothing else and looks around the room.

Ethan gets back from the bathroom and sits back down next to me. "I miss anything?" he asks, smiling at Paul.

"I was just telling Elliot that Paul didn't give him enough credit," Ricky says.

"Well," I say, leaning on my elbows and dragging my hands through my hair, "Paul also has not met me or even seen a picture of me before tonight, so it would've been quite hard for him to give you any information at all about me." Ethan kicks me under the table and I excuse myself outside for a minute.

The air feels nice and I don't feel as suffocated as I did inside. I hate going and doing this shit for Ethan. He knows I do, too, so the least he could do is pair me up with a guy who is remotely like me; I wear scarves, but I don't throw them over my shoulder like I'm walking down the runway, and I don't twirl my straw around my lips like I'm sucking on the tip of some guys cock.

I'm sure Ricky is a nice guy, but too nice to know that Ethan is just after his friends dick.

I walk back into Gregor's Pub and sit back down.

"Needed a quick smoke," I say. I don't smoke, but the lie works and everyone smiles.

The food is here shortly after and before anyone even says anything, I start plowing my face to the point where I couldn't speak even if I wanted to.

"Taste good, El?" Ethan asks, glaring over at me like I'm a kid at McDonalds making a scene because I didn't get the toy I wanted.

"Yeah," I say with my mouth full. I look over at Ricky and he looks uncomfortable, but still smiles. I try to make the best out of the situation and say, "So, what do you do, Ricky?"

"I cut hair," he says. "Well, I make miracles happen really. Some of the people that come in there. Just wow."

"A haircut does make the man," Ethan says, smiling again at Paul.

Paul doesn't talk much. Actually, Paul doesn't talk at all and all Ethan has done is ask me questions and smile like a rabid-dog at Paul the whole night.

"So what do ***you*** do, Paul?" I ask. Paul's eyes widen like a terrified newborn kitten and he just shrugs his shoulders and awkwardly smiles at Ethan. Ethan says nothing in response and continues to smile at Paul. I feel like I've just watched Frankenstein's monster come alive for the first time except this monster is really attractive and doesn't have bolts in his neck.

"Ethan," I say, "can I see you outside for a minute?" Ethan lets out a heavy sigh and meets me outside a few minutes later.

"Look," he says, "I know you are probably pissed at me right now, but just like another half hour and I'll have him locked in."

"Ethan," I say, confused, "I'm pretty sure the guy is retarded."

"Yeah," he says, "maybe, but look at him. I mean, at least God blessed him with his looks. And Ricky is cool too. You guys seem to be hitting it off." I raise my eyebrows and look up at the sky trying to find a clue to give to him. "Okay, so maybe not, but just another half hour I swear and then you can be done."

Ethan walks back into the bar and I look back up at the sky, thinking of things I will demand of him tomorrow after he is properly satisfied by the box-of-rocks sitting across from him.

I finish off my burger and play around with my fries. Gregor's always has the best food; Ethan at least picks good places to have these dates of his. It would be nice if it wasn't a place that we frequently go to together with our friends, though, because then I'm forced to remember great nights like these.

"How about you, Elliot?" Ricky asks me. "What do you do?"

"I work at a publishing house," I say. "ProjectSimpleton. It's been around for a good while now. I've worked there since my junior year in college."

His smile widens and he says, "It's so hot when a guy is intelligent. I mean, I despise reading and books in general, but I love when other people do it." I stare at him blankly, but his smile doesn't waver.

"Yeah," I say, looking around for our waitress. "I like a guy that is intelligent, too. I really like a guy that cracks open a book once in a while." Ricky's smile slowly leaves his face and I think I've made him uncomfortable finally to the point where he's lost interest. I look down at my watch and see that Ethan has five minutes left and then his half hour is up.

"My last boyfriend was intelligent," Ricky says. "He was a bottom, too, so it would've never worked anyway."

"You're a bottom I'm assuming," I say.

"One of the best," he says, winking and finishing off the last gulp of his water.

"Well damn," I say. "I am too sadly." I lie because I know his interest will fall fast and it works.

"We are all bottoms at heart," Ethan says, winking at Paul.

***Three minutes left.***

The waitress brings over our checks and I see that she put Ethan and I's on the same one.

"I forgot my wallet, friend," I say, looking over to Ethan. He knows I'm lying, but he doesn't want to make a scene. "No problem, buddy," he says. "I don't mind doing favors for others."

He looks at Paul who lays out a hundred-dollar bill for his ten-dollar meal. Stupid and rich: exactly what Ethan looks for in a partner.

"Well this was nice," Ethan says, grinning from ear to ear. "Paul, would you mind walking me home?" Paul grins and gets up from the table, grabbing Ethan's shoulder.

"It was nice meeting you, Elliot," Ricky says. "Sorry, but I just can't date someone like me. It's exhausting really." I get up and search through my wallet for some extra ones to leave for a tip. I also try to process the fact that Ricky thinks I'm like him in any way, shape or form.

"Yeah, you too. We are just to similar I think." I shrug my shoulders and shake his hand. He flips his scarf over his shoulder again and struts down the walkway towards the door. I roll my eyes and throw some ones on the table for the tip.

"That was brutal to even watch," I hear to my left, as I make my way toward the door as well. It is Hadley, Ethan's sister and my confidant in all aspects of life.

Hadley is a little under six foot tall with fiery-red hair and a perfectly symmetrical rack.

"I didn't even see you there," I say, giving her a hug. I sit down on the barstool next to her, and say, "You just get off or something?"

"Like an hour ago," she says. "I've been watching you. You've looked like you were going to die from boredom since I got here."

"Thank you for rescuing me, bitch."

"And distract you from that princess you were sitting across from?" she says, throwing her hair over her shoulder. "I wouldn't dare. Cute scarf, though. I should've asked him where he got it."

"He loved me until I lied and told him I was a bottom."

"But you are rarely a bottom, right? God, it's sad that I know what role you prefer."

"I know," I say, resting my head on my hand, "but that was literally the only way I knew to get him to lose interest and not ask me to go home with him. Also have you had a cock in your ass recently? Doesn't always feel amazing, so yes, I would much rather take the opposite role."

"You gays and your craving for the cock," she grins, tipping her beer back. "You're too picky, El."

"I'm not picky," I say. "I just don't 'crave the cock' as you put it."

"If you say so," she says, letting out a heavy sigh and looking over her shoulder.

"What?" I ask, already knowing what comes next.

"You know what," she says. "It's been over a year."

"This isn't about Drew."

"It's always about Drew and you know it."

Drew and I had been together for three years and out of nowhere, he broke up with me for no reason besides that he couldn't do it anymore. I would've been satisfied with the fact except he uprooted his life to go live back home in Indianna this past year and I haven't heard from him once since then. Plus, when he broke up with me, he could barely speak and was crying hysterically which made it even more confusing.

"You're thinking about him right now, aren't you?"

"Only because you just brought him up," I say. "I did hear he was back in town." Hadley's eyes wander and dart away as soon as they make eye contact with mine. "What is it?"

"I ran into him a couple days ago at the grocery store," she says. "It was awkward and I wasn't going to tell you because we only said a quick hey and then I hurried off." My stomach drops a little and all I can do is nod. "I can't look at him the same after he just left you hanging the way he did. Such a prick."

"Oh well," I say. "I'm pretty tired so I'm going to walk back to the apartment. I hope Ethan's enjoying himself."

"Elliot," she says, "I didn't mean—"

"You're fine," I say, kissing her cheek. "I really am just tired. I'll see you tomorrow, yeah?" She nods with a smile and I make my way out of the pub.

My apartment is three blocks east of the pub, but I take the longer route so I can stop and sit by the water on my way back. The bridge sits just north of the bench I like to sit at and the mixture of the sound of light traffic and the fish kicking in the water at night always calms me and makes me feel at peace.

Like most nights, no one is around except for a few couples walking by to go to the diner open twenty-four hours just a few blocks past the bridge. No one walks down this street unless they are planning on going to the diner.

I sit down and lean my head up towards the sky. There aren't a lot of stars because the city is right across the bridge, but if I angle it just right, I can make out a few and see planes passing by that are entering and leaving the city.

Drew being back in town does bother me. Three years is a long time to just up and leave when everything was perfectly fine. Well, things weren't perfectly fine in reality. We were losing interest in each other and I honestly got to the point where I was just living with him day to day. But the fact that he just up and left still hurts.

He has no social media, so I couldn't creep on him or see if something did happen. I was left in the dark and still haven't found a good way out of it. Him being back only leaves me with more questions and I hate the fact because even though I don't want him back, I still want to know what exactly happened.

"I thought I was the only one who came here to think," I hear to my right. His voice brings me out of my thoughts and I'm relieved that Drew leaves my mind.

"I'm usually here later in the evening," I say. "After midnight."

The stranger sits down on the bench at the other end. The city lights make his features shine in the dark and I take in every detail of him. His hair is jet black and he is wearing a fitted vest over his silver button-up. His whole outfit is fitted to the point where I could probably make out the lining of his underwear if he stood back up and turned around.

"Sorry," he says. "I'm probably invading on your you time or something." He laughs and runs his fingers through his hair.

"No," I say, "you're fine. Kind of relieved you came when you did, honestly."

"Because you've been waiting for your next kill or..."

"Definitely," I say, laughing. "Nothing like a good looking guy to get my knife out of its holder."

"Good looking, huh?" he says.

"Shit," I say, "sorry. I forget that not everyone is a homo. If you hate the gays then let me get a good five seconds to run first."

He laughs and puts his hands behind his head. "Not everyone, true. Some of us are, though." He winks at me from the side and it sends a shock through me. Could the night actually be getting better?

"My name is Will, by the way," he says, as he lets out his left hand, still resting the right behind his head.

"Elliot,' I say, returning the gesture. My eyes wander from his face to the city lights again.

"Amazing view, isn't it?" he says. "This is honestly one of the only places I can come and truly let my mind escape me." He lets out a deep breath and closes his eyes.

"Rough night?" I ask, turning to my side on the bench.

"Rough week," he says. "I'm a professor at an off branch of the college here. This fall semester has just been exhausting. If I have to read one more paper this week about why boyfriends cheat or why technology is a godsend, I will probably quit."

"You don't agree that technology is a godsend?"

He looks at me, smiles and turns his body sideways. "Not when the paper is about the great impact it has had on filtering your selfies and letting you befriend makeup artists on Instagram. I don't understand some of the younger generation or why all of these kids are going to college in the first place. I mean, I'm not ***that*** old, but still."

"She sounds like she is going places," I say, leaning on the backside of the bench.

"Oh, ***he*** will go far I'm sure." He laughs and leans his head up towards the stars. "So, how about you, Elliot? What do you do to make this world a better place one idiot at a time?"

"I'm an editor at ProjectSimpleton. It's a publishing—"

"Publishing house," he interjects. "Yeah, I have a colleague that has worked with you guys for one of her books. Marcia Avery?"

"We love Marcia," I say with a tad too much excitement. "I love her work and she has made the business a pretty penny."

"How long have you been working there?

"Six almost seven years now," I say. "Started my junior year in college. How long have you been teaching?"

"Six, actually," he says. "I started as I was going through the process of my masters and it stuck. I was good at teaching and English was my favorite thing to learn, so I thought, why not?"

"Not your dream job, I'm guessing?"

"Don't get me wrong," he says, "I do love it. I love when a student actually gets the stuff I'm teaching and when I have that one person in the class who really shines because they love the subject matter so much. That never happens anymore, though. Today's youth just doesn't care as much; they are there because they're told it's the only way to be successful."

"Maybe you just don't have the drive you had before?" As soon as I say it, I know it might offend him. I get too personal and comfortable too quick and I say whatever feels right. "Sorry, I didn't—"

"No," he says, nodding, "you're right. I mean, a lot of things have made me not love it as much anymore, but I mostly just don't strive to teach anymore, sadly." I look over at the bridge and see flashing lights; there must've been a wreck.

"That looks bad," he says.

"I'm sure there is worse that has happened tonight in that big, beautiful city over there."

"Probably," he laughs. "I'm sure a few unsuspecting people were murdered while sitting on a bench with a total stranger tonight."

When Will laughs, his smile widens and he shows his perfectly formed, beautiful teeth in the process. Everything about him is nice, I realize, as I slowly take in a new detail every other second. His jawline wide and masculine and his eyes are perfectly symmetrical with the width of his nose.

"Is there something on my face?" he says, wiping his palm across his cheeks.

I laugh and can feel the redness in my cheeks and say, "No. You're just nice to look at."

He looks from me to over my shoulder down the road.

"Do you want to get a bite at the diner down the road?" he asks me. "I'm starving." The thought of eating more food makes me want to puke after I practically swallowed everything at the pub.

"Sure," I say. The thought of spending more time with Will is nice, though, and he hasn't murdered me yet, so I might as well talk with at least one guy who may interest me tonight.

***

"Wait," Will says with a mouth full of fries, "are you seriously telling me the guy didn't talk once while you were at dinner?"

"Not once," I say. "He just smiled a lot and then almost passed out when I asked him a question."

"Jesus, man," he says. "I'm sorry." He makes a pouty face and takes a bite of his burger. "And your guy wasn't any good either?"

"Not my type, no."

"And what is your type?" He rests his chin on his hand and his smile widens.

"Random strangers I meet on benches at late hours of the night," I say. "Good looking ones who share my interest in murder jokes."

"I have to say," he says, "I never in a million years thought I would meet someone on a bench and be sitting with them at the diner down the street. Nothing like a love story that doesn't start on a hookup app."

"Love story, huh?" I ask, circling my finger around the rim of my glass. His face reddens and I instantly smile when his eyes shy away from mine. "Love stories have a hard time of finishing with a happy ending in my relationship history."

"Maybe you just haven't found the right character to have a happy ending with," he says. "I understand, though. It's easy to fall in love, but it's hard as hell to accept falling out of it."

"I bet you really know how to unintentionally make the students swoon over you when you teach them. You have a way with words, William."

"Bleck," he says, craning his head back. "The only person that calls me 'William' is my mother and it turns into William Henry Everett because it's only when she is mad at me. That and my sister does the same thing sometimes."

"That's cute," I say. "It's better than Elliot Edison Edwards."

"Oh my god," he says, laughing. "I'm sorry, but that is just mean. It's nice, though. Can I refer to you as 'Triple E' at parties and such?"

"Ew," I say, putting my hands in front of my face, "no. I had a boyfriend in high school who called me 'Triple E with the long, thick D' and, needless to say, it didn't work out."

"That's creative," he says. "Also interesting, depending on how much fact goes with the name." My insides chill and I feel my dick move just a tad, as he looks at me with his dimpled smile.

"Well," I say, "maybe after a few more diner dates I'll satisfy your curiosity."

He looks at me with his head titled, biting on his lower lip.

"Good," he says. "I respect a man that doesn't put out on the first date."

You don't even know how bad I want to.

Will looks down at his watch and says, "I hate to do this, but I have to get back home. I have grades to put in before three am and it's almost one. Are you going past Walker and fifty? I live around there."

"Yeah, I live on forth, actually. I'll walk you. Well, you can walk me I guess."

We get up and as I go to open the diner door to leave, Will opens the door before me and his hand grazes my back. My body tightens and I feel a chill go through me. When his hand leaves, I instantly want it back.

"So, this is weird," he says, as we make it a block down from the diner.

"What is?" I ask.

"Tonight," he says. "Not that I haven't enjoyed it. Honestly, I'm really glad I met you, but it's just the oddest thing, isn't it?"

"No," I shrug. " I do this all the time. Meet hot strangers on the park bench by my favorite view of the city, eat with them at the diner and then have them walk me home. Literally, every night."

"Shut up," he says, shoving my shoulder, and I feel the chill again. Every time he touches me, it feels good I'm learning.

"I mean, yeah," I say, scratching the back of my head, "it's random, but the best things in life happen when you least expect it, right?"

"Let's hope so," he says.

Three blocks later and we are outside my apartment building. The lights off in Sam's room, so I'm guessing he is asleep. I really didn't want Hadley to be the first one to hear about how the rest of my night went because I could already sense the overenthusiastic reaction I would be greeted with in the morning.

"You're good to go the rest of the way?" I ask.

"I'm a big boy, Elliot," he mocks. "So…"

"Am I going to see you again?"

"In my dreams tonight," he says, sticking his tongue out. "I'll call you and we will set something up? Maybe something a little fancier than a diner this time and a softer place to sit and talk besides a bench."

"That bench will forever be our spot though, ya know?"

"I can't wait to tell our kids the story."

He embraces me for a hug and a chill instantly runs through my body. I wrap my hands around his back and feel the outline of his muscles as he breathes in and out. His scent is delicious and I basically inhale his shoulder, as I rest my head on it briefly. I find comfort in his arms and I don't want him to let go.

"Ok," he says, letting go and making my insides ache a little. "I'm going to go home and think of ways to better sweep you off your feet while I devour my work stuff, so be prepared to be wowed next time we talk. Which will be sooner rather than later. Because I like you."

"You're alright, too, I guess." I smile at him and, turning on his heel, he smiles back.

I get into the apartment and Sam is asleep. He has his drawings laid out over the kitchen table and I have to stop and marvel over them. I met Sam through work because he often does work with our authors for their book covers. He does amazing work, but wants to branch off into more things entertainment-wise. The drawings on the table are from his partnership with a new TV show pilot that, if successful, could launch his career exponentially.

Whether it works out or not, Sam's talent doesn't go unnoticed and he will always have the publishing house if he needs it because they love him there.

I turn off all the lights and make my way to the bathroom. I pop my toothbrush in my mouth and the only thing on my mind is Will. I've talked to guys before and hit it off quick - it's easy if they can carry a conversation. Will is different, though. Even when he randomly showed up while I was sitting by the water, it wasn't weird. It felt welcoming and comfortable; that is weird. It takes me weeks to feel remotely comfortable with any guy. So why was Will so different?

You're overthinking it.

Just as I go to spit my rinse out, it hits me. He said he would call me, but we didn't exchange numbers.

Fuck.

# Chapter Two

Will

"WHAT DO YOU MEAN you didn't get his number?" Lydia pauses with her fork in the air and slings a piece of pancake to the floor. Since birth, Lydia has had a flair for the dramatic. When I was born, my mother said that Lydia stood with her arms crossed, one foot tapping, and said, "That's what everybody has been so excited about all these months?" and stormed out of the hospital room.

Gotta love them sibling bonding moments.

"I thought we did, honestly," I say, shrugging. "I mean, I even told him at the end of the night that I would call him and everything. Then I get home and right after I'm done brushing my teeth, it hits me."

"You know where he lives, though, right?"

"Yeah," I say, "but I don't know which apartment is his."

"Then sit outside on the stoop like some psycho until he either comes home or comes downstairs."

If it was any casual encounter then I wouldn't care, but Elliot was interesting. I wasn't even looking to talk to someone that night, but he was there and it was easy. And he was ridiculously attractive: his black hair was thick and shiny. All I could imagine was tugging on it while we went at it. His eyes were a glossy emerald color and his teeth glistened against the city lights.

"Seriously, Will, you need to see this guy again. I haven't seen you light up like this in awhile. Damn it, Abbey." Lydia's two-year-old daughter Abbey is every uncle's dream. She is adorable when she is with me and a hellion when she's with her mom. I love it.

"I'll figure it out," I say. "I'll sit on his stoop if all else fails. I mean I got his last name and everything."

Lydia cleans the seat where Abbey dropped her scrambled eggs and looks up at me and says, "Then Facebook him, what are you waiting for?"

"Shouldn't I give it a day or two?" I say. "I don't want to seem overly eager and scare him away."

"What if you wait and he finds a new guy on a new bench and goes to a new diner in a new city?" I roll my eyes at her and she smirks. "Look, all I'm saying is you make him seem like someone worth being eager for. Give it the weekend if you want. Go to your show tonight and then tomorrow, find his ass."

"My show," I mock, rubbing my palms into my eyes. "I didn't even think about that. I hate getting all suit-and-tied up for this stuff. I always feel funny."

"You always look damn good and you know it," she says. "You feel uncomfortable because you aren't comfortable with how good looking you are and it is annoying. Why do you think they have you stand up there and give all the big speeches?"

"Because I'm the head of the arts and science division on campus?"

"No," she says, "because you are nice to look at and people love throwing their money at pretty people. Probably because of your work stuff, too, but just saying. What's this event about anyway?"

"Young readers overseas," I say. "All the money collected is going towards shipping more books overseas. A lot of publishing houses around the city are donating some of their stuff to give them an idea of what is getting sent over. The same thing I do every year."

"Exciting stuff, bro," she says cleaning Abbey's face with her napkin. "Isn't it Abbey? Isn't Uncle Will just the coolest person ever?" Abbey looks up at me and her smile instantly sends a rush of love through me. The thought of having my own child is nonexistent at this point because of work, but being the uncle of all uncles is just as worth it.

"Are you guys doing anything exciting tonight?" I ask, finishing off the last of my waffle.

"Watching NickJr and going to bed at eight," she says. "Switch ya?"

"I'd love to hang out with Abbey. I don't know why you're hatin'."

"Try pushing her out of your vagina and shitting all over the table and having her cry every time she doesn't get her way at the store so she screams and it looks like I torture her. Then tell me how much you adore her."

"You win." I scrunch my face at Abbey and she heaves with laughter.

***

I go the grocery store after I leave Lydia and Abbey. I've fallen into the same routine this past year and each day it gets exceedingly more boring and pathetic.

Every Sunday I have breakfast with Lydia and Abbey, which I love doing, and then I go to the grocery store, which I despise doing. Then home to do whatever schoolwork needs done before Monday and then, with whatever time I have left, I plan out lessons way ahead of time or read myself to sleep.

Basically, Sundays suck in the Everett household; except today. The event later and the thought of seeing Elliot again are a welcome change. Assuming I see him again.

"Will?" I hear behind me, as I reach in the cooler to get a gallon of milk. My stomach instantly goes sour and drops to depths I'm not sure I knew existed. I turn around and standing in front of me is Miley: Evan's younger sister.

"Miley," I say, as she gives me a hug, trying not to let my un-comfortableness show. "How are you?"

"I'm doing good," she says. "Really good. I've tried to get ahold of you a lot since last year."

"I know," I say, looking down at the floor. "I just haven't been able to move past it. Seeing you guys just makes it resurface in ways I can't explain and it's not something I think I'm ready to fully handle."

"I get it," she says, smiling, "really. I still think about him everyday. It gets easier. You knew him in ways we didn't, though, so when you're ready, just know we are all here for you. We miss you." She waves and makes her way down the isle. My legs feel like they are going to buckle and I lean against the cooler door for balance.

Why today? Out of nowhere.

It all comes flashing back to me; each vision worse than the one before. I was doing better and thought I might finally have been moving past it.

"Are you ok, man?" I hear the man beside me ask, bringing me out of my haze. "Wait here and I'll go get some—"

"No," I say. "I'm fine. I just got dizzy for a second. Nothing is wrong, but thank you." I turn the shopping cart and make a path towards the exit. I speed up the closer I get until finally, I abandon the cart completely and shove it to the side by the registers. I can feel everyone's eyes on me as I storm out of the store, but it doesn't faze me even a little.

I make it to my car and fumble with the keys. I drop them and, as I go to reach for them, I slam my head into the side of the car. I don't feel it as it hits, but I frantically grab the keys and unlock the door.

I slam the door as I sit down and plant my hands on the steering wheel, squeezing tighter than my blood circulation can allow. My breathing slows and I slouch back into the seat - sweating and exhausted.

I debate whether or not to go back into the store and get what I needed in the first place.

I'll probably need to switch grocery stores now.

I wasn't expecting, of all things, to see Miley. I have made it a priority to stay away from his family because they didn't see what I did, besides his mom, and they weren't there in time to say goodbye. I don't know whether it's for me or for them at this point that I've forced myself out of their lives.

I start up the car and drive to the store in the opposite direction of home.

***

I take a detour home and drive by Elliot's place. I don't know why, but the thought of him calms me and brings me back down to where I need to be. I've never met a guy and after only one night been infatuated with the idea of having him in my life. I can't tell if he is home or not because I have no clue which apartment is his, but I can't help and wonder if he is in there thinking about the lack of a phone number he has, too.

Maybe I shouldn't be getting into something serious so soon, though.

Or maybe that is exactly what I need already.

***

I drop my keys on the counter by the door and immediately fall into the couch once I reach the living room. I have to speak at the benefit around nine which leaves me three hours to either nap and half-ass it, or make myself the perfect gentlemen.

I choose a mixture of both and lazily get up and make my way to my bedroom. I open the sliding closet door and roll my eyes once they make contact with the suit I wear to every special occasion that I rarely want to attend.

This benefit is for an amazing cause, but getting all dressed up and fake-like makes it seem like more of a show then anything. A "Does the wallet match the label?" kind of night where I have to shake hands and kiss ass just so they'll feel entitled enough to donate their money for causes they probably care nothing about. Or maybe I'm just being a pessimist.

My mind wanders back to Elliot as I lay out my suit on the bed. Over the course of the year, I've talked to other guys, but I would never get close to any of them. I always felt guilty, like I was cheating on Evan, which I know isn't realistic, and that they would sense that it was going nowhere and lose interest.

I never let it get to me because I was OK with being alone. After the one-year anniversary, though, I realized something had to change. Maybe Elliot could be that change for me, even if we just became friends at least. Or maybe I'm overthinking it again.

Black tie or pink? Maybe bowtie would go better with the suit. I'll figure it out once I get the damn thing on.

I go in the bathroom and wash my face. I've always had decently healthy skin and the aging process hasn't hit me to hard, but I still like to take precautions to keep myself presentable.

My hair is greasy and disgusting from all the sweat produced during my meltdown earlier, so I put my head in the tub and lather it up; letting the follicles soak for a few minutes before I rinse. I usually part it to the side, but tonight, I slick it back and mat it down with some gel.

I put my contacts in and refill the solution casing. They hurt at first because I haven't worn them in a while and the adjustment is straining. I wear glasses because it makes me feel less noticed and more sophisticated.

Once I get everything but my jacket on, I sit on the bed and wonder what to wear with it. Everyone will be wearing black and white, so the more reason to wear pink. Tie or bowtie is the question. Tie is more professional, but bowtie would make me seem more carefree which may be more attractive to some people. It could also do the opposite and make me not look professional.

Bowtie it is.

I put my jacket on and look one last time in the mirror.

It will have to do.

Driving to campus, I go by Elliot's again. No lights are on in any of the apartment windows and I don't know what car he drives to see if he is home. I will have to creep on his doorstep tomorrow after classes, that's all there is to it. Unless I just go to where he works. He did tell me he works at that publishing house.

A shred of relief goes through me and I instantly feel stupid. I'm thinking about this guy like a high school kid in love for the first time and I'm overthinking things. Sometime this week, I will just go and show up at his work, because I'm crazy, and he will either be pleased to see me or have me escorted out.

First time for everything I guess.

***

The campus parking lot and streets are covered in nothing but metal. Car after car, and I start to wonder just how good the donations will be tonight. Even though my passion for teaching has faded, my passion for helping the less fortunate, especially when it comes to education, hasn't faded one bit.

I go to the staff parking lot which thankfully has a spot open - even though it is the farthest from the entrance doors. I lock the doors and focus on my breathing, as I make my way to the dining center where the event is being held; not that I get nervous about the idea of having to give a speech, but you can easily stumble over your words when faced with a crowd just dying to give you their money.

"Good evening, Professor Everett," a former student of mine says, as I make my way to the doors. "You're looking quite dashing this evening."

I laugh and say, "Well thank you, Pete. You're looking pretty snazzy yourself." I always got the impression that Pete had a crush on me when he was a student of mine. Not because he was in fact gay himself, and made sure to make the fact known in conversations quite often, but because he would bite his lip when he talked to me one on one and smile.

"What are you doing here?" I ask him.

"I actually work with the company heading the benefit," he says. "I'm going with the group to take everything over once everything is ordered. It's pretty cool, honestly, because I want to travel." He looks over my shoulder and then back to me, biting his bottom lip. "In large part to you, Mr. Everett."

"Well," I say, checking my watch, "I'm glad I could inspire someone. That's my goal here." His gaze doesn't waver and the unease is starting to set in. "It was good to see you, Pete. Hope everything goes as planned."

"Me too," he says, his gaze still unwavering.

I make my way through the entrance doors and start walking towards the stage they have set up. The stage is rounded with a different exhibit every few feet of promotions and reasons to provide for the event. The curtains to access behind the stage are red, draped in gold, and the stage floor is laid in black.

I look around at my surroundings and see table after table laced with pamphlets and information about the publishers attending the event tonight. The tables are all laid in black as well, and the pamphlets are drenched in red and gold. To top it off, there is a small candle in the center of each table with an inscription carved on the side of the holder. Each one recognizes a quote from a famous author and education in general.

I recognize a few names off the list, but once I skim further down the list, my eyes focus on a single name: ProjectSimpleton

My heart immediately starts racing and I look around like an idiot to see if I can spot Elliot anywhere. I think he said he was a lead editor, so most likely he will be here attending.

I make my way over to the display stand for ProjectSimpleton and look at the names displayed for attendance along with a picture of the people. There are three names: Andrew Simpson, Elliot Edwards, and Samuel Erickson. I look at Elliot's picture and smile because the picture doesn't do him justice. His smile is gorgeous and I realize that his relaxed, laughing smile is the same as his forced, fixed one. It looks like a recent picture because he is sporting the same haircut he was when I saw him the other night.

"We need you backstage, Will," I hear to my right. Standing beside me is Missy who is the coordinator for the whole event and one of the leads on the organization in general. Educate-Us-All has been designed from top to bottom by Missy and without her, it would be nowhere near as successful as it is now.

"You're looking pretty sharp tonight," she says.

I straighten my bowtie and throw her a smile and say, "Got to impress the bank accounts, right?" She laughs and checks something on her iPad that I can't read clearly.

"Damn it!" she says. "Adam is late and we need someone to go confirm who from the publishing houses is here." My eyes grow wide and I feel my body tingle.

"I'll go do it," I say, as calmly as I can. "Just tell me what I need to know."

"You already have enough to do, Will," she says. "I don't want to overburden you with extra stuff."

"Really," I say, smiling, "I don't mind at all. The prompter has my speech and other than that, I just have to mingle and look pretty, so it's nothing."

She takes a second to think and then says, "If you're sure. Just remember, I gave you a choice and I'm not bossing you around and instructing you to do this for me. You chose to do this for me because you're awesome. Everyone thinks I'm a bossy bitch, so I want to be clear that you are helping out of the kindness of your heart." She looks me in the eyes, not letting her serious expression waver.

"I offered because I'm amazing. Got it." I nod to her with an expression as serious as I can make it and she busts out laughing.

"Come on," she says, "and I'll show you where they all are." She arches her head over her shoulder towards the hallway and I follow.

We make our way through the Science Department of the campus and into one of the larger lecture halls. As we make our way through the door, I suddenly feel myself get nervous and anxious. I can't tell if it is a happy nervous or an 'oh-shit' kind of nervous. I'm not sure how to react once I see Elliot besides overly enthused and crazy.

As we make our way down the stairs leading to the desk at the center of the room, I don't look around me, but instead focus my attention between the desk and my feet. If Elliot is in here, I don't see him.

"Here is the list of the publishing houses," Missy says, as we turn the corner of the desk. "There are either two people or three from each house here to present and speak. Here is the sheet with the order they are presenting in, so just ask for them from this. Just put a checkmark next to each name that is here and have one of the members sign. If there isn't at least one person from each organization here then let me know as soon as you finish. They should all be here, though, because they were supposed to come early."

I lift my eyes and do a quick scan of the room, but it's to quick to make out anyone or spot Elliot.

"Got it," I say.

"Once you're done just have them follow you back stage behind the curtain. I will be back there unless something goes wrong tonight, but let's hope not." She checks something on her iPad again and smiles up at me. "Thank you again, Will. If you weren't gay you'd be a dream guy for us ladies."

I smile and say, "Well maybe one day they will make the cure. I'll keep you posted."

"You're a dork," she says and makes her way back up the stairs.

I call off each publishing house and ask them to come to the front to have them sign in and give them a rundown of what will happen when they go up on stage. Eventually, I get to ProjectSimpleton

Two men make their way down the aisle and neither one is Elliot.

"Hi," the taller, gray-haired one says on the right putting out his hand. "Andrew Simpson, head of the company. And this is Sam Erickson, our lead graphic-design artist in the company."

I can already tell Andrew thinks highly of himself, but Sam seems moderately normal and laid back. He has dirty-blonde hair and green eyes and a beautiful smile when he says, "Hi, nice to meet you…"

"Will," I say, laughing, "sorry. Will Everett."

Sam's eyes grow a tad wider and I have no idea why. He looks me up and down and then smiles and says, "Nice to meet you, Will. I'm also just a freelancer with the company. Not a lead designer. Not that it matters, but yeah."

"It says here that there should be one other member of your company. An Elliot Edwards?" Sam looks at me again and grins.

"Elliot is running late," Andrew says, reminding me that he was even there. "He had a meeting with a potential investor for the house, but he should be here before the event starts." A surge of relief goes through me and I smile. Sam laughs and I focus my attention back to the task.

"Ok," I say, "you guys are the last ones so that should be it." Every other group I had leave once I registered them in, so I escort the other two out and we make our way back to the event area.

"I know who you are," Sam says, nudging my shoulder. "I'm beyond glad you are here."

"Why is that?" I ask, bewildered.

"Elliot hasn't shut the fuck up about you since he met you the other night."

# Chapter Three

Elliot

"FUCK!" I MASH MY HORN AS the two cars in front of me go twenty miles under the speed limit. I am already late for the fundraiser and slowly getting more pissed as the time passes.

The meeting with the investor was a bust and he wanted to basically demolish the company and revitalize it into a whole different genre than what we specialize in at the publishing house. My phone lights up in the cup holder and I see it is from Sam.

***You will never believe the special guest they booked for the event tonight. You are gonna lose your shit.***

I didn't hear about any special guest when I was going over the event with Andrew. It was supposed to be pretty low-key, but still swarmed with the richest people in the city. People that Andrew frequents with: assholes.

When I started at the company, Andrew was into his third year and already on his way to running the place. His dad had part-ownership of the house before he eventually sold out so Andrew got the job at exactly the right time. Every day I hope that someone slams into him with their vehicle while he is walking down the block on his way to work with his morning coffee in his hand and his phone pressed to his ear, not paying attention.

He is the biggest asshole in the whole city and the day he makes a mistake, his job is mine.

I drive through the campus gates and make my way to the parking lot. Everyone has already arrived and there isn't a parking space in sight.

I drive around and up to the student parking lot, which is a mile away from where I need to go, and park in the spot closest to the walkway. I lock the car and make my way down the staircase leading to the actual campus. The stars are out in full tonight and as I look up to admire them, my pant leg catches on a hook protruding from the side of the bar that goes all the way down the walkway. It takes me by surprise and I trip over my feet and fall down a few steps - tearing my pant leg and getting covered in dirt.

Now I'm irate.

I finally make it to the entrance doors and I am greeted by a guy who is a good bit younger than me and looks like he is still in high school. He smiles as we lock eyes, but it fades the closer I get.

"Are you OK, man?" he asks me.

"I'm fine," I say, as calmly as I can. "I just fell down. Did it start already or am I good?" He looks me up and down again with a mixture of confusion and interest. I snap my fingers in front of his face a few obnoxious times and he zones back in.

"Yeah," he says, "you're good. Go on in."

I walk through the door and make a right towards the bathroom. The only thing that could make tonight worse was if the water wasn't working in the bathroom. I rush past an older guy and his wife, well probably his wife but it is hard to tell, and make my way to the sink in the bathroom.

A damp paper towel gets rid of most of the dirt and I fix my hair back to what it looked like before I fell. I tuck the ripped part of my pant leg into my shoe.

Ugh.

"What the hell happened to you?" I hear behind me and I jump. I look in the mirror and see Sam's reflection laughing at me with his hand pressed against the bathroom stall.

"It hasn't exactly been the best evening for me, dick."

"How did the meeting go?" he asks.

I give him a thumbs down and say, "He wanted to change everything about the content we publish. Wanted to keep up with the times and do what everyone else was doing."

"Vampires and erotica?"

"Basically," I say. "Did you find out what we are doing here as far as presenting?"

Sam's smile widens and I scrunch my face in confusion.

"What?" I ask him.

"We are presenting last," he says.

"That has you smiling because..."

"That isn't why," he says with his grin still wide. "You'll see why. Let's go."

Sam leads me out of the bathroom and down the hallway towards the eating area where they have the event set up. There are weird mixtures of black and red and gold podiums set up in a circle around the stage with each publishing houses' info that is attending the event. The room is filled with people that I will probably never see or speak to again and I instantly feel suffocated and annoyed by all the shoulder-bumping going on, as I make my way towards the back of the stage.

As I brush past an older group of gentleman talking about their summer plans, my eyes skim to the left most side of the stage where I see a photograph of a familiar face kneeling by two children; a photo, it looks like, from past years when they had actually went overseas.

My heart starts racing when I see the name at the bottom of the photograph: Will Everett.

"Holy shit," I say, grabbing Sam's arm and jerking him back to where my feet are firmly planted. "It's him."

Sam starts laughing and says, "I know. I met him earlier." My eyes shoot to Sam and he starts laughing even more.

"When did you meet him?"

"He was doing the check-ins earlier for all the different companies presenting tonight. He played it cool when he saw your name, but I could tell he was nervous and then disappointed when you weren't there. I'm soooo glad you got his last name."

"Did you tell him I was coming?" I say with a little more force than necessary.

"Yes," he says. "Calm down, Elliot. Your boyfriend is expecting you so don't get all psycho-crazy now." I roll my eyes at him and he redirects me towards the back curtain.

We walk through and the number of people is almost half of what it was on the other side of the curtain. My eyes immediately scan the room to see if I can spot Will, but they dart too fast and I can't really make out anyone.

Sam grabs my arm and jerks me out of my daze and to the left to where Andrew is waiting for us. He doesn't even speak and I'm already over being in his presence and wish he wasn't here attending in general.

"Elliot," he nods with a smirk, "you look worn-out this evening. Meeting didn't go as planned?"

"Not a good choice for the company, no."

"Well, anyone with money they are willing to invest is a decent choice if you ask me, though."

"I didn't," I say.

He raises his eyebrows at me and his smirk widens as I say, "Maybe next time you should send one of your less inclined workers to have the meeting with him." Sam grabs my arm and jerks me to the left and we walk to the back of the room.

"Really, Elliot?" Sam says.

"Fuck him," I say, shaking my head. "The sooner he moves on to something else, the sooner the company can be made into more than a fund for stupidity." I look around the room to see if I can spot Will, but still nothing.

"What are you going to say to him when you see him?"

"Who?"

"Will," Sam slowly says, raising his eyebrows.

"I don't know," I say. "I haven't really thought about it."

"Well, you better think quick," Sam says, pointing over my shoulder to the back of the room.

As I slowly turn, there stands Will, head to toe flawless, in his suit. He isn't wearing his glasses like before and I can make out details in his face that I couldn't before with them on. His nose has a perfect curve that settles well with his face shape and his eyes are a bright blue that makes my insides quiver. His hair is pushed back and shiny and all I can imagine is having a handful in each of my hands while I sit on top of him, riding him deeper and deeper into me. I shake back into reality before I get overly involved in my fantasy and wonder if I'm truly going crazy since my first thought was being his cum-dumpster.

As I look back up to where he was standing, I see he is gone.

"Where'd he go?" I ask Sam, suddenly annoyed.

"He has to go present I think," he says. "He is the main headliner for the whole thing; being the head of the department and all that." I look around the room and don't see him anywhere. I look down at my watch and see the event officially starts in five minutes.

"Good evening, everyone," I hear over the loud speakers. "My name is Will Everett and I will be, well, I guess your host for the evening. Basically the guy that stands up here and looks pretty for you and tries to sway you into giving me all of your money." The crowd of people laughs and then Will proceeds to laugh into the microphone.

"All joking aside," he starts, "everyone here running the benefit is beyond thrilled that you all could make it here tonight and it truly is for an amazing cause that I have been apart of since I was younger and started going to when I went to school here myself. The program has a special place in my heart and for those of you who are new to the event this year, I'd like you to please take a moment and enjoy this short video that we have scrounged up for you all. Thank you."

The video starts playing and it's a collection of pictures and moments from past years when groups have gone overseas. I see Will come back through the curtain, off the stage, and I instantly freeze when he tilts his head up and his eyes lock with mine. For a second, I don't think he recognizes me because his stare turns hollow and blank, but then his grin grows wide and his gorgeous smile glistens in the light. My heart instantly starts racing and all the negative energy I had bottled up from the day leaves me instantly. He shakes a few hands and makes his way over to me.

"Before I forget," he says, pulling a piece of paper out of his wallet. He hands me the paper and I see it has his phone number written down. I slowly look up to him and smile.

"Hold on," I say, taking out my phone. I put his contact info into my phone and create a message. I click send and wait for it to ring in on him.

I hear a ding and he reaches for his phone - his smile not wavering and his eyes never leaving mine.

"I'm glad you are here. Mostly because I was going to resort to just going to where you work and asking for you like a jealous boyfriend or something. That or just sit on your steps until you came home or left."

"How romantic," I say, winking at him. I feel a nudge from behind and I turn to see Sam smiling at me. "Will, this is Sam who you have already met, I think."

"Yes," Will says, nodding. "He told me that you haven't shut up about me since we met." I turn to Sam and glare.

"Sam is my roommate and ex-best friend," I say.

Will laughs and says, "I loved the fact that you haven't stopped thinking about me. I'd be concerned if you did. The video is ending here soon and I am literally out there while everyone speaks. I'll talk to you once all the presentations are done?" I nod and he smiles, turning around and heading through the curtain again.

"Why would you tell him that?" I instantly ask Sam.

He scrunches his shoulders and says, "He loved it. When I said it, he lit up earlier. It was cute, but also kind of sad. He seems like he is really interested in you. Why I don't know, but I'd say he is crushing just as hard on you as you are on him."

I punch him in the shoulder and smirk.

***

After an hour of bullshit speeches and all the houses promoting their new works, Will finishes with a closing speech and then tells everyone to enjoy the rest of their night.

"Remember," he says, "the higher the amount on your checks, the wider the smiles on the children's faces that we help." He takes his fingertips and stretches them on each side to emit a wide smile. Everyone laughs and then proceeds to clap as he makes his way down the steps towards the bar area. I say excuse me to the group we were sitting with and make my way over to him.

He sits down on the bar stool and runs his left hand through his hair. I can see him let out a big sigh as he plants both palms straight into his temples.

"Excuse me, sir," I say, placing my hand on his shoulder, "but may I bother you for an autograph." He looks up at me, already smiling.

"I'm so glad that is over. I love the purpose of all this, but hate being the speaker for it."

"You did great," I say. "Not a dry pair of panties in the room." He laughs and takes a sip of the wine he ordered.

"So," he says.

"So," I reply back with a nod.

"It's a little crazy we're both here tonight, right?"

"Fate," I say with a wink. "I had a terrible day today, so yeah, a tad crazy that it got this good."

"Why?" he asks. "What happened?" He rests his head on his right arm and he focuses in on my face.

"Just a bad client meeting and my boss is a douche and I fell walking to the building."

"You fell?" he questions, giving me a once-over with his hand. He waves it up and down and laughs.

"Down the steps by the upper parking lot. My pant leg caught and yeah."

"I've did that before," he says, laughing. "That wasn't a good day at all for me or my students. I think I actually made one of them cry that day."

"I don't see you being a mean teacher at all."

"I can be," he says, "but rarely. Sometimes you just have to let the aggression out and sometimes that aggression gets let out on annoying college students who care way too much about why they got a B plus on a paper instead of an A."

"I was never like that," I say. "As long as I passed, I could care less, but I still did good, I guess."

"Same," he says, taking a big gulp of his wine. "I always hated being in the classroom. Still amazed that I'm a teacher because of the fact."

"What got you into teaching?" I ask him.

"Someone inspired me to," he says. "Long story. Better for another time I guess."

I grab his glass of wine and take a sip. I don't take my eyes off his the entire time and neither does he mine. I can feel them going through me - trying to figure out what exactly I'm thinking. If only he knew how bad I wanted to let him taste the wine from my lips and take him on the counter space right here and right now. I take another sip and set the glass back down in front of him - slowly licking my lips in the process.

"Good choice," I say, tilting my head to the side. I see him swallow and he rearranges the way he was sitting.

Did that of all things get him hard?

"So, what are you doing after this?" he asks, circling his thumb around the rim of the wine glass.

"I have a lot of work to get done before tomorrow," I say. "Honestly, the meeting today was unexpected and was thrown on me last minute and it's just been chaotic ever since I got the message from Andrew this morning." I see his expression turn serious again.

"He did seem like a bit of an ass when I met him. Not that he said much, but you sometimes get those vibes from people, ya know?"

"Good judge of character you are."

He laughs and finishes the rest of the wine in his glass.

"What is it anyway?" he asks. "About him that hits a nerve?"

"He is just the head of something that he shouldn't be. I guess it's a mixture of annoyance and envy. If he wasn't here right now, I would have his position and the company would be doing a lot better than it currently is." I plant my elbow on the counter. "One day, I guess."

"Is that your dream? To run ProjectSimpleton?"

I stop for a moment and let my mind wander.

"No," I say, "but it's what I have worked hard for all these years and I already do most of the work, anyway, so I know I'm good at it."

He smiles and lets out a small laugh.

"What?" I ask.

"Most people would pout and say screw it, but you are determined. I like that."

He sits up straighter and asks the bartender for another glass of wine.

"I like you," he says. "At least, I like what I've learned so far."

"You must really like me if you were going to come to my office and be all stalker-ish," I joke. "I can't say much. I was going to look you up on Facebook if all else failed."

"Same," he laughs. His smile, even without much light, can still be made out and it warms me; excites me.

"What are you doing Tuesday night?"

"Shouldn't have anything going on," he says.

"How about dinner? We can decide where tomorrow or something. Now that I have your digits."

He laughs and says, "My digits? You're cute. Nothing would please me more than to see you on Tuesday night. Seeing you in general is never a bad thing, I'm learning."

"Same," I say and he laughs again. "It's a date then."

"I haven't been on a real date in forever."

"Me either to be honest," I say. "I dated one guy for a good while and once that ended, I wasn't too keen on seeing anyone else again."

"Until you met me and all my awesomeness," he says.

"Basically," I say. "I like you with glasses just as much as without them by the way. A lot of people can't pull that off."

"Really?" he asks. "I don't like myself without them on to be honest."

I see his face frown for a split-second before he looks up at me and smiles again.

"Because they make you feel smarter?"

"Exactly," he says. "That and I feel like people take me more seriously when I wear them. I'm not just a pretty-face when I have them on if that makes sense."

The fact that Will isn't completely comfortable with his looks surprises me. He is gorgeous, but I guess that is the point. There is more to him than his pretty-face.

"Is that another reason you don't love being the host at these things?" I ask.

"Yeah," he says, focusing in on my eyes. "I just wonder if when I'm presenting in front of all these people if they see an intelligent, successful college professor who has accomplished a great deal, or if they see a piece of eye-candy that is used to help boost the number of zeros on the checks. It helps the cause I guess, but it stills feels shitty when I walk around and talk to random people and even flirt with some others just to get more money out of them. These people love having their asses kissed."

"Well," I say, "honestly, I just see eye-candy, but I'm sure there is something under all that pretty." I wink at him and he lightly kicks my leg with his.

"All caught up are we?" I hear Sam say behind me, as he sits down to my right. He flashes his smile and orders a drink while eyeing the bartender.

I look over to Will and he starts laughing.

"Elliot asked me out on a date," Will says. "I said yes, but I'm starting to have my doubts."

"I don't blame you," Sam says and I roll my eyes.

***

Will and I make our way up the stairs to where my car is. Everyone who didn't leave the benefit at this point is just there to help clean up and Will was nice enough to walk me back to my car.

"Another year down," he says, as we get halfway up the stairs.

"How many years have you been doing this?"

He thinks for second and says, "Nine or ten I think? I started late in my freshman year as far as helping, but I started doing more and more through the years."

"That's dedication."

"I enjoy the helping aspect of it all," he says. "Honestly, going overseas and seeing kids faces light up just because they get a book to read is heartwarming. I cried the first time I went over because I was so moved by it all. They have nothing and something as simple as a book gives them a sense of purpose."

"But you don't go over anymore?" I ask.

"No," he says. "There are enough volunteers now that the program has gotten bigger and I don't really need to. Plus, it's miserable over there."

He laughs and says, "I envy my showers and air conditioning too much."

"Let me give you a ride down," I say as we make it to my car. "You have to help clean up right?"

"Benefits of being the speaker is that I'm not expected to help out," he says. "But yeah, I will go help out anyway because that's just me."

"What a gentleman you are," I say.

"Cute ride," he says, as we get to my car.

"What's cute about it?" I say, laughing.

"The driver," he says.

He laughs and puts his seatbelt on. We make our way out of the parking lot and I feel every bump in the process.

"Are they ever planning to fix this or no?" I ask.

"Probably not," he says. "The campus is looking into adding an extension onto the Arts and Sciences building because of the large number of Liberal Arts students who apply, so all the money is basically focused on that for the time being."

"That will be nice," I say, as I pull into the circle that sits in front of the cafeteria entrance.

"We'll see," he says. "I don't know what department it's aimed for, but I know it's not English. It will probably just be a new computer lab or a bigger tutoring center which would be nice."

He lets out a heavy sigh and tilts his head back.

"So, Tuesday then?" I say.

He turns to me and sits upright in his chair.

"Tuesday," he says with a nod and a smile.

He goes to open the door, but stops midway and shuts it back closed.

"Before I forget," he says, sliding over closer to my seat.

He takes his right hand and puts it under my chin. Slowly, he moves his lips closer to mine and with my head tilted back, he kisses me and takes my bottom lip in his mouth. He takes his other hand and runs it through my hair and kisses me again. I lock my tongue with his and pull him closer into me, taking the back of his head in my hands.

Every emotion in my body amplifies and I want nothing more than to have him in the backseat right here and now. I move my left hand from the back of his head, down his chest. I make my way down to his pants and grip his massive bulge in my palm. He moans and I feel him harden more under my grip, as I massage him back and forth.

"Ok," he says, biting my bottom lip and moving away from me. "I need to get out of the car before I get naked and have you in the backseat."

"What's wrong with that?" I say, smiling up at him.

He kisses me one last time and gets out of the car.

"I'll text you once I'm done here. Give me like an hour probably. Bye, stud."

"Bye," I say, as he slowly walks backwards smiling. As I make my way out of the gates and onto the main road, I see my phone light up in the cup holder.

***I'm still here, obviously, but I couldn't wait and had to go to the bathroom and finish what we started. I couldn't walk otherwise.***

As I make my way back home, all I can think about is Will in the cafeteria bathroom, thinking about me while he comes all over his chest or the toilet seat or whatever he felt the need to glaze, and I can't wait to get home and finish what we started myself.

# Chapter Four

Will

IT'S TUESDAY AND I have no idea what to wear for this damn date.

Sitting on my bed is a mountain of clothes that I either think are too dressy or too casual; I also haven't been on a date in years and have no idea how to act on one at this point. Even though two nights ago we made it past the comfort level of casual, I'm still nervous as hell.

My mind flashes back to that night and the utter torment I felt having to get out of Elliot's car. If I wouldn't have, I would've taken him right then and there, though, and fucking in a car isn't my idea of the best first time with a person.

Especially someone like Elliot who I want nothing more than to sprawl out with on a bed and go at it for hours on end.

"Hello?" I hear, as the front door shuts closed. I make my way into the kitchen and see Lydia getting a glass of water.

"What's up?" I ask.

"Tonight's the big night so just wanted to make sure my baby brother picked out something nice to wear for his new boyfriend." Lydia smiles and I roll my eyes as I sit down at the table.

"It's a disaster in there," I say, pointing to my bedroom. "I'm almost to the point of asking him how he is dressing so I don't over or under do it."

"Jesus, Will," she says. "Are you in high school or what?" She leans off the counter top by the faucet and sits down across from me at the table. "It's almost sad watching you run around like a little girl. Don't be a pussy."

"I just want to make sure I look good."

"He's already seen you, though, so why is what you're wearing an issue? Next you'll be worrying about whether or not you'll kiss well the first time." I scrunch my face and bite the side of my lip.

"What?" she asks.

"Nothing," I say. She crosses her arms and focuses in on my face. "Maybe we already did a bit of that the other night after the benefit." Her eyes grow wide and she slowly shakes her head.

"You forgot to mention that when you were telling me about seeing him again."

"I know," I say. "It was a bit out of character for me; initiating it and all."

She laughs and says, "Yeah I would say so. Will Everett is never the one who would usually jump into making out with a guy he has only known less than a week."

"I can't help it, Lydia. When I'm around him, I feel different. Every emotion in my body heightens and I just want him."

"Good," she says. "That's a good thing."

"But then I think about—"

"Do not say you think about Evan," she says. She gets up from the table and puts the glass in the sink. She turns around and leans against the counter again and says, "I'm sorry. I just don't want you to use that as a reason not to find someone new. Whether it is Elliot or someone else. You shouldn't be alone."

"I don't mind—"

"No," she says. "Will, you have literally pulled away from everyone but me. You go to work, come home, run and then focus more on work. It's not healthy and you need someone else to talk to besides me." She lets out a sigh and says, "I heard about the other day at the store. I talked to Miley."

I shake my head and scrunch my shoulders and say, "It was nothing."

"Then why did you storm out of the store after you saw her. She wasn't sure if you were pissed or what the hell was going on."

"It just brought up a lot of things. Images I didn't want to see and sounds I didn't want to remember hearing. It was fine, I just had to get out of there."

"I get it," she says, walking over to the table again. "I don't know. If you need to talk about it let me know, but don't let that stuff ruin things for you with Elliot. Even if it doesn't work out, at least you put yourself out there again."

I look around the room and think about the day I moved out of the house because it was no longer my home. It was Evan and I's home and I no longer felt comfortable there.

"Where are you guys having dinner at?" Lydia asks, drawing me out of my haze.

"Gregor's Pub," I say.

"And you are wondering what to wear?"

"It's not like I'm picking out a suit and tie, Lydia, but I still want to look good."

"You could probably wear a dirty shirt and sweat pants and he would still want you. Especially if you gave him a taste already."

"Shut up," I say, laughing.

"Just try and enjoy yourself tonight. I know you guys already have talked before and had a sit-down, but this is different."

"Thanks, mom."

***

I get to the pub and see Elliot sitting in a booth towards the bar-area and I instantly smile. He is wearing a button-up with the sleeves rolled back, and light jeans that make him look like a hot, young college kid and I let out a soft moan. I need to focus tonight and not picture him naked the whole time or I'll make things awkward.

"Hey," I say, nudging his shoulder as I get to the booth.

He instantly lights up with a smile and gets up and hugs me. Instead of a quick hug, he pulls me in tight and I can smell his body wash and my nose grazes the side of his neck.

"You smell good," I say.

"So do you," he says, letting go. "I'm starving. You've been here before you said?"

"Yeah," I say. "In college, mostly, but haven't been for a couple years."

Not since Evan.

I put the thought of Evan out of mind and sit down in the booth across from Elliot.

"You look cute tonight," I say.

"Yeah," he says, scratching the back of his neck. "I wasn't sure what to wear honestly."

"Can I get you guys some drinks?" The waitress says, as she gets to our booth. She is checking her notepad and leans on one hip. When she lifts her face and makes eye contact with us, she instantly gushes when she sees Elliot.

"Yeah, Val," Elliot says, "I'll just have a coke and then whatever Will wants." He nods to me and Val gives me a onceover. Her smile heightens and she bites her lip a little.

"Coke is fine for me, too," I say, smiling.

She scribbles something down on her notepad and says, "I'll be right back."

She winks and turns around, flipping her hair to the side, as she strolls back to the bar-area.

"Friend of yours?" I ask.

"Not really," he says. "She has worked here for a few years, so she knows me and I her, but we aren't biffs or anything."

"She basically got down on her knees ready to service you when she looked into your eyes," I say, teasing.

"Is someone jealous?" he says, tilting his head.

"I'm sure I'll have the opportunity one day."

His eyes grow wide and he laughs and says, "Damn, already at it with the flirting and we haven't even had something to drink yet."

"You like it," I say, laughing.

"I do, I do. How have you been since we last saw each other?"

"I've been OK," I say, scrunching my shoulders. "Just been grading and preparing stuff. You?"

"Same," he says. "I mean I haven't really did much besides plot Andrew's demise."

"Oh, can I join?"

"Gladly," he says, winking. Val brings our drinks and sets them on the table.

"You guys ready to order or need some time?"

"Shit," Elliot says, "sorry. We haven't even looked at the menu yet." He looks up at her and frowns like a sad puppy dog.

"Oh, that's alright, honey. I'll come back in like five." She smiles and goes to the next table.

"So," I say, "what's good here, *honey*?"

"Well, *babe*," he says, "they have good subs and fries. Or the pizza is good if you want to split that. Or the classic burger and fries is always a good choice."

"A sub sounds amazing right now. Can you get the fries loaded?"

"Yeah," he says, smiling. "I always get mine loaded with cheese and bacon. Best thing ever."

Val eventually makes her way back and takes our order. She doesn't give Elliot any new pet names as she leaves and walks back to the kitchen.

"So, did you grow up around here or come for school?" he asks.

"Lived here all my life," I say. "My older sister lives a few miles away from me and she basically took care of me growing up. Our dad died when I was three and my mom tried her best, but ya know." His eyes focus on mine and I look down and say, "What about you?"

"Yeah," he says. "We moved around the state some, but always around this location. Just couldn't leave the city I guess. What's your sister's name?"

"Lydia," I say, smiling. "She's my rock basically."

"My parents only ever had me. But I don't know. I see Sam and Ethan as brothers. And Ethan's sister Hadley is like my rock."

"How is Sam?" I ask. "Did I pass the friend test I mean?" I laugh and he smiles.

"Yeah," he says, "you passed. He thought you were great."

"He seemed pretty cool."

"Sam is the friend that likes everyone basically until you give him a reason not to. It's Hadley that is somewhat of a tough-one. She has literally never liked one of my boyfriends."

"Jeez," I say, tugging at the neckline of my shirt. "Should I be worried?"

"No," he says, laughing. "I just say that so when I introduce you to her you don't think she is a bit of a bitch because she comes off kind of mama-bear like."

"And Ethan?"

"Ethan?" he says, resting his hands on the table. "Ethan is Ethan. He is a man-whore by day and an even bigger man-whore by night and will probably hit on you the moment you meet him." He takes a sip of his drink and laughs. "Ethan has been my best friend since freshman year, though, and I love him to death. He just can be a bit much sometimes. He had a rough relationship a few years back and it kind of escalated from there I guess in a weird way."

"That's never good."

"What about you?" he says. "Your sister, I mean. Will she be a tough one to crack?" He smiles and takes another drink of his coke.

"No," I say. "I think she'll like you. Even if she doesn't, I like you. Mostly just the way you kiss, but your personality is pretty good, too."

"Same," he says.

Our food comes and I can feel my mouth water as I take a bite of my sub. I moan a little and look up to see Elliot smirking.

"What a nice sound that was," he says.

"Sorry," I say. "It's just so damn good."

"I told you," he says with his mouth half full. "This place is fantastic."

"So, tell me something about you that would surprise me."

He thinks for a minute and puts down his fork and says, "I worked as a stripper a few towns over on the weekends when I was going to school. I made enough on the weekends to pay for everything I needed to live while going to school so I never had to work during the week."

"That's surprising," I say.

"I win," he says, laughing. "What about you?"

"Before I decided to teach, I had planned to drop out of school all together."

"Really?"

"I didn't see the point of it and spending thousands every semester that I would eventually have to pay back made me not want to even more."

"So," he says, "what made you decide to teach then?"

"I was overseas doing the program and I met this young kid. He was around ten probably and he knew some English, but not a whole lot. After I did a reading, he came up and asked me some questions and then asked me certain specifics about our language and how to use certain terms. Teaching him those things made his face light up and I ended up giving him my personal textbook from way back when I took an intro class on writing. I liked seeing that need to learn in him and wanted more of it."

"And now you wish you hadn't started teaching?"

"Kind of," I say. "I mean, I still like teaching and enjoy helping people learn, but I'm over the atmosphere in general I think. Maybe I'll try stripping."

"Are you going to tease me about that forever now?" he says, laughing.

"Of course," I say.

I finish off most of my sub and start picking at the rest of my fries. Elliot is a fast eater I've learned and practically inhales his food rather than digest it.

"I got an offer to go overseas," he says. "Over to London to head a publishing house over there. It's a new company and they haven't produced a lot of works yet, but they really want me to come over and takeover as head of it all."

"That's awesome! What did you tell them?"

"I haven't said anything yet," he says.

He plays with his fork and his expression becomes more serious.

"I don't know," he says. "I mean it would be awesome, but all my friends and family are here and I'm close to running where I am now."

"Yeah," I say, "but if you went to London you could already be in charge of something. Obviously they see something in you that hasn't been appreciated by where you are now." He looks from me to the table and back at me. "How long do you have to decide?"

"They gave me a few months. It wouldn't happen until early next year anyway. It's an extension of where I work now mostly. Andrew has been talking to them and I've been working things out and getting to know the people. I'm terrified he's going to fuck it all up for me."

"You have plenty of time to decide then. I'm sure it will all work out."

"Yeah," he says. "Sorry, I don't know why I randomly brought that up. I haven't told anyone about it yet."

"No one?"

He shakes his head and takes a drink of his coke.

"I know if I told my friends they would all say how I would be stupid not to do it."

"It's whatever you want to do. If you went to London, I could visit you and have a reason to leave the country." I wink at him and he nudges me under the table.

"That was delicious," I say, wiping my mouth.

"I love it here," he says, smiling. "I've never brought a date here, though."

"Why not?"

"This is like my home away from home, I guess. I've been coming here forever and there is always at least one person here that I know and can talk to. Bringing dates here just seems like an invasion or something. That makes no sense, I know."

"Why'd you bring me here then?" I ask, smiling.

"I like the way your tongue tasted in my mouth," he says.

"Same," I say and we both laugh.

"No," he says, "honestly, you're different, I guess. I feel unrealistically close to you having only known you a week. Almost like a love at first sight kind of thing. Not that I love you. I just really like being around you."

"Well, I love you," I say. "I was going to propose and everything tonight."

"Shut up," he says, kicking me under the table.

"No, I get it," I say. "Honestly, I feel the same way. You've been a breath of fresh air into my life and I'm grateful."

He smiles and leans his head to the side. I can see his phone light up across the table and he looks down at it. His smile fades and his face grows serious.

He throws his head back and sighs.

"Apparently Ethan is in the hospital," he says.

"Is he OK?" I ask.

"Yeah," he says, shaking his head. "He got into a fight and broke his nose and now he needs a ride home and of course it is me because Hadley would kill him."

I can't help but smile at him being angry.

"You're cute when you're pissed."

He looks up at me and smiles.

"I'm sorry," he says. "I feel like such a dick right now."

"It's fine," I say, getting out my wallet. "It was a date regardless."

"No," he says, "I'll get this one. The least I can do."

We walk to the parking lot and he leans against the side of his car with his head arched back.

"I'll text you once I get all this settled tonight. I'm sorry again."

"It's OK," I say, leaning against the car next to him. "Thanks for getting dinner."

"Of course," he says.

I turn to my side and look into his eyes. I take my right hand and cup it under his chin. I slowly bring my mouth closer to his and tilt his chin up, as I make contact with his lips. He grabs the back of my head and runs his fingers through my hair with one hand while the other is still planted against the car.

I lean off the car and stand directly in front of him, placing both hands on his face and palming each side. He moves his hand from the car and pulls me closer from behind as I dig my tongue into his mouth.

**"BEEEEEEP!"** I hear, just as Elliot leans back more, and the car alarm scares us both.

"Well," he says, laughing. "I guess that is a sign that I should get going."

I take my thumb and wipe his bottom lip. I give him one last peck and move back away from him.

"Tell Ethan I said hello."

"Oh," he says, "I will tell Ethan many things once I get to the hospital, I can assure you."

# Chapter Five

Elliot

"DO YOU HAVE YOUR key?" I ask Ethan, as I practically carry him to the door.

"Here," he says, handing me everything in his right pocket including his keys. I sit him down against the side of the walkway and try three different keys before I get the right one.

"Come on," I say, throwing his arm over my shoulder.

I kick the door shut behind me and we slowly walk to his bedroom. I lay him face up on the bed and take off his shoes.

"Elliot," he says.

"Yeah."

"I'm sorry."

"It's fine. Will says hello by the way."

"No," he says. "I mean about this. About calling you."

"I'm used to it," I say.

"I know." He arches his arm above his head. "I'm sorry."

Ethan zones out halfway through his second sorry and I sit on the bed and run my hands up my face and through my hair. The phone calls rarely happen, but when they do, there is always something broken or he is always passed out to the point where I have to take care of him.

I walk into the bathroom and get the small trashcan and bring it to Ethan's bed. I go back into the bathroom and damp a washcloth and put it on the nightstand for when he inevitably pukes during the night.

Ethan's past has directed him in ways I can't fathom. Rick alarmed me from the start, but Ethan saw something in him that we didn't. I know he won't remember tonight, but something has to change with him. Seeing him wreck himself week after week is getting old and it's to the point where I wonder if I should get him help myself.

I make sure everything is turned off and that he has room to breath under all the covers and make my way back home.

***

"Was I bad last night?" Ethan asks at breakfast the next morning.

"You need to stop this shit," I say. "I'm not just saying that because you ruined my date. I know life hasn't been the kindest to you, but you're going to get yourself killed."

"Agreed," Hadley says. "I love you baby brother, but you're a fucking idiot when it comes to men." Hadley sticks a piece of her waffle in her mouth and wipes her face with her napkin. "How was your date by the way, El?"

"It was great," I say. "Cut-short sadly, but great."

I give Ethan a glare and he frowns.

"Have you gotten any yet?" Ethan asks with sausage in his mouth.

"What does he do again?" Hadley asks.

"He's a professor. He doesn't seem to love the fact, though."

"What do you mean?"

"He just seems unfilled," I say. "He enjoys it, but it's not what he wants to be doing."

"Speaking of being fulfilled," Hadley smirks, "I met a new guy a couple weeks ago and it seems to be going well so far."

"Have you gotten any yet?" Ethan asks blankly. Hadley stares at him until he smirks and goes back to eating his food.

"What's his name?" I ask.

"Ed," she says.

Ethan starts laughing and almost chokes on a piece of sausage.

"Please tell me it is Ed Johnson from high school," he says.

"Yes, Ethan, it's that Ed."

"Oh my god this is fantastic news," he says. "Elliot, this guy is the dumbest person on the planet. Hadley dated him in high school."

"We aren't even talking about dating here," she says. "Just enjoying each others company."

"So you're fucking?" Ethan says.

"He isn't as dumb as he used to be. He's actually a major head at one of the big law firms in the city."

"Is that how you guys met back up?" I ask. "Through work?"

"Yeah," she says, smiling. "I was working a case and had to go to court to speak as a witness for the arrest and he was there representing the victim. We went out for drinks and yeah."

"Isn't it frowned upon to date people like that in your field?" Ethan says.

"Ethan," Hadley says, closing her eyes.

"I'm just saying," he says.

He turns to me and says, "When are you seeing Will again?"

"Soon probably," I say, shrugging. "I haven't talked to him yet today, so we haven't made any plans to meet up. Do you want to tell me what you were doing last night that landed you with a broken nose?"

He looks out the window to his left and then looks down at his eggs.

"Not really," he says.

"Why?" I ask him.

Ethan never has a problem talking about his wild nights out.

"I was on my way home from the bar and I got jumped by a couple of guys. I didn't have anything on me so nothing was taken, but they did mess me up a tad." Ethan looks up at me and his eyes are wet. "It was easier to let you think that it was just another small bar fight like every other time I've called you."

He looks down at his plate and scrapes around the rest of his food and says, "It just brought up stuff I guess and it's not something I wanted to revisit."

"He can't get to you anymore," I say, grabbing his hand.

"I know," he says, pulling away. "I have to go. I have a day-date later today with Paul."

"Seriously?" I ask.

"What?" he says.

"That guy is an idiot."

"What he lacks upstairs he more than makes up for downstairs. Truly, I think he was designed with the intention of having sex and that's it." Ethan stands up and wipes crumbs off his pants.

"Sister, dear," he says, kissing Hadley on the head.

"So," Hadley says, looking me in the eyes.

"What?" I ask.

"You seem different the past few days. Since you met Will, I mean."

"Is that good or bad?"

"Good," she says, smiling. "You're smiling more at least."

"I like him," I say. "I mean, I know I haven't known him for very long, but I'm comfortable with him already I guess."

"And he feels the same way?"

"I don't know," I say, laughing. "I assume since he is still talking to me."

"When can I meet him?" she says, tilting her head.

"I don't know."

"How about tomorrow night?" she says. "I don't have a lot of work to catch up on so I'm completely free."

"I'll ask him," I say, pulling out my phone, "but just you. I don't want to run him off. Plus it's a little early in general for him to meet anyone. I now nothing about him myself yet."

"I can't fucking wait!" she says and I shake my head at her.

***

"Running a little late are we?" Andrew says as I sit my bag down behind my chair in the office.

"I told you yesterday I would be coming in later."

I'm already annoyed with him and it isn't even lunch yet.

"I know," he says, laughing. "I'm just messing with you. I have a client coming in later today to discuss possibly setting up another office on the west coast. It looks to run smoothly as long as we can find someone to go over and start the process. I'm thinking Amanda would be a good lead over there. What do you think?"

"I think whoever you feel would be best equipped to run a whole new department on the opposite side of the country should probably have a good bit of experience and not still eat lunchables everyday at lunch." He smirks and leans against the doorway. "Have you considered going over yourself?"

"I agree that I would be the best one to go over."

Not what I meant at all, but all right.

"I couldn't imagine leaving everything here in the hands of someone else, though," he says. "Honestly, I don't know what this building would do with out me." He rolls his eyes and crosses his arms.

"Something else you need?" I say, raising my eyebrows.

He shakes his head no and walks out of the office. He stops at Amanda's desk on his way back to his. The only reason he thinks she is a good fit is because he knows his dick is a good fit inside her pussy. Not that I want to go anyway, but if Andrew would take it upon himself to go, that would let the opportunity arise for me to handle things here.

Andrew would never allow that, though. He knows I'm good at what I do and that I should be where he is.

I look down from my computer screen to see my phone lit up.

***I'd love to have dinner with you guys. What time? ☺***

Will's use of a smiley face makes me smile and all the annoyance from Andrew quickly fades away.

***8? I'll let you know where at once I talk to Hadley.***

***OK. Maybe we can finish that kiss after?***

The memory pops into my head from last night. His tongue was practically down my throat and then the car alarm went off.

I feel my pants tighten in the crotch and try to focus on something else.

***Can't wait. ☺***

The meeting with the client doesn't go as Andrew had planned so the rest of the afternoon he is in a shitty mood which only worsens my mood. Having such disdain for a human being makes me feel like a terrible person myself, but I can't help it; Andrew is the worst.

I focus on the rest of my work and think about seeing Will again. My negative thoughts start to vanish and positive ones of Will and Will's mouth take over.

***

"So, Elliot told me you are a teacher?" Hadley says to Will, as she hands her menu to the waiter.

Will is wearing a gray button down with an even darker shade of gray pants. The top two buttons are open and when he reaches over to grab his drink, I can make out little tufts of chest hair protruding from the opening.

"Yeah," he says, smiling. "I used to teach at the university itself, but they needed a department head at the off branch outside of the city, so I transferred over."

"I don't know how you guys do it," she says. "You're basically the back-bone of the country and you don't get paid nearly enough."

"Well the good ones don't usually do it for the paycheck. But I mean it's just like you and your career. You risk your life everyday and the pay isn't the best."

"Not about the paycheck," she says, laughing. "Knowing I'm helping people makes up for it I guess."

"How touching," I say, resting my head on my hand.

"Elliot wouldn't understand," she says. "He just gets paid to sit around and read books all day."

"And I'm damn good at it if I do say so myself."

Will's grin grows and his beautiful smile makes my heart skip a beat. For a second, I get lost in his smile and then my gaze focuses on Hadley's who is staring right through me practically with glee.

"Here you guys go," the waiter says, as he sets down our drinks. "Is there anything else I can get you for now?"

"We're good, thanks," Will says, smiling up at him and I see the guy blush a little. Will's looks and charm would make even the straightest man do a double take.

Hadley notices me gazing at Will again and clears her throat. I glare at her.

"Any plans for the weekend, Will?"

"Yeah, actually," he says back at her. "I'm flying down to South Carolina for a work thing Friday morning. I was actually going to see if Elliot wanted to go with me."

I instantly feel elated.

"Like the beach?" I ask.

"Yeah," he says, laughing. "We would fly back Sunday night and I'm only busy Saturday during the beginning of the day, so we would have all weekend to do whatever. It's all paid for by the university except for food and stuff."

"That sounds like a great little vacation, El," Hadley says with a wink.

"It does," I say. "I'd love to go. I should be able to get Friday off. Andrew doesn't want me there anyway."

"Good," he says. "I have a crap ton of miles so don't worry about the flight."

"You don't have to—"

"Don't worry about it," he says, shaking his head. "You can just pay me back with your company."

My mind wanders to us sitting on the beach and his bottom lip in my mouth. There's no one around, so we are undressed and I make my way from his lips to his stomach and finally to his cock. I can feel it throbbing as my tongue touches the tip and he lets out a soft moan.

"Elliot," I hear Hadley say, as she brings me out of my fantasy.

"Yeah," I say, switching positions in my seat and I instantly turn red. Will looks at me with curious eyes and I smile at him. "What were you saying?"

"I was telling Will about your freshman year when you and Ethan ended up in that basement at that gas station."

"That was awful," I say.

"How does that even happen?" Will asks, laughing.

"Too much alcohol," I say.

"You puked all over my car that night. I hadn't met you yet. It was your guys' first weekend there."

"And the last weekend I ever blacked out again."

"Oh come on," Will says. "That's the last time you ever partied? Your first weekend of your freshman year?"

He crosses his arms and tilts his head to the side, smiling.

"I swear," I say, putting my hands out in front of my chest.

"It really is," Hadley says, laughing. "From there on out it was babysitting Ethan which surprised me. I figured they'd both be a handful, but Elliot wasn't like my brother thank God."

"How is Ethan by the way?" Will asks me, taking a drink of his water.

I throw at quick glance at Hadley.

"He's good," I say. "He just had a rough night all together, but he's good."

"My brother doesn't tend to make the best decisions in life," Hadley says. "But he's a good guy. He just needs a good guy to rein him in and keep him in check."

She puts her arms on the table and says, "You don't have a gay brother by chance, do you?"

"No," Will says, laughing. "Sadly not."

Our food arrives and it's delicious. Like she always does, Hadley beats her fork into one of my cheese-filled raviolis and moans as it slides down her gullet.

"I'm glad you like it," I say, shaking my head.

"I never get the right thing when we come here. These damn Italian restaurants and their thousands of ways to cook a noodle."

"You always enjoy what I get," I say. "A sane person would just get that the next time."

"But then I can't try something else, Elliot. What if I like this new thing even more, but because I didn't try the new thing, I miss out?"

"You guys are cute," Will says, taking a bite of his Alfredo. "This is delicious by the way."

"Yeah," Hadley says, moving her fork around her plate. "Elliot got that a couple weekends ago and I loved it."

Will looks at me with a smile and I start laughing.

"Two good places in a row, Elliot," Will says. "What's your secret?"

"I'm trying ***really*** hard to impress you."

"Oh whatever," he says, laughing.

"My mom always said the quickest way to a man's heart was through his stomach," I say, resting my chin on my hands.

"Your mom also has been divorced four times," Hadley says.

"Yeah," I say, "but she is a damn good cook."

"That she is," Hadley nods. "I miss your mom. She needs to come to the city so we can go dancing again."

"That was a ridiculous night," I say, laughing. "Watching her grind on Ethan was something I will never get out of my system."

"She is obsessed with Ethan," Hadley says. "She told me that night that she sits in bed every night just sad about the fact that he is a homosexual."

Will's laughing and Hadley smiles at me as I glance from him to her. I see her look down as her phone buzzes and lights up on her lap.

"Sorry, guys," she says. "It's work." She gets up from the table and heads to the bathroom.

"I like her," Will says, still laughing. "She's good people."

"She's pretty great," I say. "A lot more relaxed than I thought she would be. I figured she would be watching you like a hawk, but I think she likes you."

"Good," he says, "because I don't plan to go anywhere anytime soon."

He winks at me and finishes off his water and says, "You really want to come with me this weekend then?"

"Of course," I say, instantly lighting up. "You made my day with that offer. I haven't been to the beach since I was little and a free mini-vacation? I mean come on." He smiles and purses his lips. "Plus I'll get to spend more than a few hours with you for the first time. I'd be dumb to reject that."

"I can't promise I'll be exactly ***gentlemanly*** with all this time with you alone," he says.

He moves positions in his chair and looks above my head as I hear Hadley making her way back to the table.

"Sorry, guys. I have to go. This case I've been working on just got a lead and I'm ready to find this fucker." She slings her coat over her arm and throws some cash on the table.

"It was great meeting you, Will," she says, hugging his shoulder. "Elliot, I'll talk to you later once I'm done. You guys enjoy the rest of your night." She smiles and turns toward the entrance practically running.

"She really loves what she does doesn't she?" Will asks, laughing. "I've never seen someone get that excited to rush into a dangerous situation."

"You should see Ethan when he goes to Vegas and turns on his hook-up apps. A gunshot is nothing compared to all the diseases I'm amazed he doesn't have."

"What does Ethan do for a living anyway?"

"He works with different security companies going from business to business and setting up their network systems and making sure everything is, for the most part, secure from hackers and all that. He's a really intelligent person. He just had some bad luck in the past and it messed him up in a weird way."

Will shifts in his seat and his eyes focus on his plate.

"We all have something in the past that haunts us, right?" he says.

He smiles up at me, but it isn't genuine and my mind instantly starts to wander into ideas of what he has in his past that is making him tense.

"So, you're sure about using your miles for me?" I ask, changing the subject.

His smile this time feels genuine again and I feel less tense about the situation.

"I'm never going to use them for myself so it's the perfect opportunity. It will be an awesome time. I haven't been to the beach in a while either. Once I moved here I didn't explore much besides when I went overseas and all that."

"I like the beauty of the sunset and the sound of the waves in the morning," I say. "I don't even like swimming in the damn thing. The view is the best part."

"It will be a cute story to tell our kids one day," he says.

"Just not the ***whole*** story, right? Or are you planning to be a gentleman now once we are down there?"

"Oh," he says with a laugh, "right. I wouldn't say I ***plan*** to do anything because that makes me look bad in a sense I think, but if an opportunity arises, I don't think I'll be able to control myself.

Every time I've had your mouth on mine, something ends up ruining the moment and I'm left with tight jeans and a throbbing dick and it's so uncomfortable."

"Same," I say. "I guess we will just to see how things go down there, yeah?" I finish off my glass of water and lick the wetness from my lips. I focus in on his eyes. "I wouldn't be against the fact if you did have some plans for us this weekend, though, I can promise you that."

# Chapter Six

Will

"JUST BE CAREFUL, WILL," Lydia says, rinsing off the rest of the dishes from breakfast.

I wave my hand in front of Abbey's face while we are sitting on the couch watching cartoons, but she is so completely zoned in to the point where I think she can see through my hand.

"There is nothing to be careful about," I say. I make my way to the counter top in the kitchen and sit on one of the stools. "It's just a weekend getaway."

"But I can tell you like this guy and I don't want you to jump in too quick and then be devastated if something happens."

"We aren't even dating yet."

"You already have a life planned out with him," she says, "don't you?"

"Shut up," I say and she laughs. "Plus, you're the one that said I need to get out and all that."

"I know," she says. "Just take it slow is all I'm saying. You haven't known him that long and you are already taking a trip to the beach together."

I agree with her. It probably is a bit much, but I like his company. I like him. He relives any tension I have no matter my mood and the sound of his name makes my smile grow from ear to ear, and a smile hasn't rested on my face in awhile.

"I'll be careful," I say. "How are things here?"

"Good," she says, drying her hands off. She throws the rag to the side and makes her way to the refrigerator. "Just tired. Abbey has me exhausted and Greg is never home hardly because of work."

"You guys could've came with me for the weekend. Get a break from here."

"No, it's fine. I'm glad I told you no when you asked me the other day because I'm interested in what happens with you and Elliot."

"I'm not going to lie, I hope *something* happens. I don't mean sex really either, but that wouldn't be so bad I guess."

She laughs and says, "You definitely need a good lay, baby brother. You're so tense most of the time and I hate it. I think

Elliot is good for that. I've noticed a difference in you since you've met him. Nothing major, but better still."

"It freaks me out," I say.

"What? Why?"

"I haven't wanted someone like this since Evan and it all feels new to me I guess. I mean other than Evan I had only dated a few guys and none of them really in too serious of a way."

"Don't think like that all weekend or you'll ruin it for yourself."

"I know," I say. I run my fingers through my hair and get up off the stool.

"What time does your flight leave tomorrow morning?"

"I think nine."

"Well you should probably be sure."

"It's nine. Picking Elliot up around seven-thirty. I still haven't packed."

"Really?" she says. "I figured you'd have had it sitting by your door since Monday."

"I don't know what we are going to do to be honest. I don't know what to bring to wear. Besides some trunks and a suit for Saturday."

"Does this guy dumb you down or what?"

I look at her confused.

"Just pack some clothes like you normally would," she says. "He already wants you. You don't need to impress him anymore, Will."

"I know," I say, laughing. "You're right. Jesus, I do sound stupid. I do want to impress him though."

"Then just be normal. The happy version of your normal and if he doesn't like it then you shouldn't be with him anyway."

***

"Ready to go?" I ask Elliot, as I pull up to the curb outside of his apartment.

"Since you invited me," he says grinning from ear to ear.

He puts his bag in the back seat and checks his pockets to make sure he has everything before getting inside.

"I think I have everything," he says, bringing his seat belt over his chest. "If not, oh well."

"Were they pissed that you took today off on such short notice?"

"No," he says. "Andrew made a comment about how it must be nice to take days off because he works nonstop, but other than him being his normal, cocksucker-self, it's fine."

I laugh and make my way out of the small streets towards the interstate.

"The reviews for the hotel we are at are pretty good," I say swerving into the far, interstate lane.

"Well that's good, Will," he says, laughing.

"Sorry," I say, rubbing my neck. "I don't know what to talk about to be honest."

"How's your sister?"

"She's good," I say. "She told me to be careful with you this weekend."

He looks at me and smirks and says, "Don't drop me or I'll break."

"She just thinks it's a bit weird that you are going with me this weekend. Too quick."

"Well," he says, "just think of it as new friends who really enjoy kissing each other and touching each other inappropriately getting a much-needed vacation."

He digs in his pocket and takes out his phone.

"I agree with her somewhat, though," he says. "It is really fast, but I don't know. How else are you supposed to get closer to someone?"

"I like your reasoning," I say.

"To be honest, I don't think it's weird. Maybe I'm just too comfortable around you already or something, but I am really glad you asked me to come with you. It means a lot. Especially since you are paying for the flight and stuff. Which I will still pay you for if you want me to."

"If the weekend ends up being terrible then I'll let you pay me back. Deal?"

"Deal," he says, nudging my shoulder.

***

"I have a secret," Elliot says, as I'm putting the carry-on bags in the overhead storage. "I hate flying."

"Afraid of heights?"

"No," he says, practically sewn into his seat. "I just don't understand how it all works and it freaks me out and I know these things rarely have crazy-huge problems, but you never know, you know?"

"It's only a few hours," I say, sitting down next to him by the window. I grab his palm and lock his fingers with mine. "I'll protect you in the meantime."

He stares straight ahead and takes a breath and says, "I appreciate that, but if I'm falling to my death this high in the air then there isn't much you can do for me."

"True. And I forgot to bring our parachutes, so I guess you're fucked, bud."

"It's a lot of hours from here to London," he says, looking over at me and then to the window.

"Have you been thinking more about that lately?"

"Yeah," he says. "Honestly, since I've met you, I've been thinking about the fact that they don't want me to run anything where I'm at. They are opening a new office on the west coast and Andrew already has his eyes on one of his associates going down and getting things started. She hasn't even been there that long. It's just a spite thing with him. As long as he is there, my position is set in stone and I'm not moving up no matter what."

He looks out the window and lets out a sigh.

"Not that I even want to go over there," he says. "I wouldn't even if he asked me to, but the fact that I am not the first choice is ridiculous and sad and I just need to move on and stop bitching and feeling sorry for myself. Right?"

"Right," I say. "Why did knowing me suddenly make you feel all this?"

"Because you made me realize life isn't about waiting. You have to take opportunities when they present themselves and see where things go."

He looks me in the eyes again and laughs. "Sorry, enough about me and work. Is the hotel ocean-view?"

"It's beautiful," I say. "At least the pictures look like it, but yeah, we should have a nice view of the ocean from the balcony."

"Would you ever have sex on a hotel balcony?"

I look up from my phone and look at him with raised eyebrows.

He laughs and says, "Sorry. It's like a fantasy of mine. Two hot guys fucking on a balcony with a gorgeous view and people possibly staring."

"You like it when people are watching you?" I ask, beyond curious.

"No," he says. "It just seems a little dangerous to me and I like that."

"The idea sounds nice," I say. "Depending on the positions."

"Let's say, for example, me and you are on the balcony and this is happening."

"Alright," I say, smiling.

"Let's say I'm looking towards the ocean and I have my hands planted firmly on the rails."

"Are you clothed or no?"

"Completely nude. Obviously, William, I mean come on."

"Okay," I say, putting my hands up. "Continue."

"I'm standing there and you come up behind me. You rest your head on my shoulder and kiss my neck. You wrap your hands around my stomach and squeeze into me until we are practically the same figure."

He stops and gets on his phone.

"And then what?" I ask.

"I don't know," he says. "You'll have to decide that on your own I guess."

Elliot looks over towards my crotch area and laughs. I look down and notice the firm bulge outlined through my pants. I set my jacket across my lap and laugh.

***

"Do you want to go out or order in?" I ask Elliot, as he takes out his laptop and sets it on the counter top.

"Go out of course," he says, smiling up at me. "And I'm buying so don't even argue with me on the fact. What sounds good?"

The rest of your balcony story, I think.

"Anything really. Steak sounds good."

"Steak does sound good," he says. "I'll look up a nice steak house around here. Something we don't have back home."

I go to the bedroom and set my bag on the table beside the TV. I get my laptop out and check my emails. The newest one is a schedule for tomorrow and I see that the meetings last from eight in the morning until five in the afternoon.

I jot down the address of where it's taking place and close my laptop back up.

Outside, the view of the ocean is beautiful. Outside the limits are boats and people parasailing. There are planes going by with banners advertising different stores around town and I can hear people laughing down at the beach enjoying the sun.

"I found a place," I hear Elliot say behind me, pulling me away from the beauty of the ocean.

He walks over and looks out the window with me and says, "Reminds me of the pier back home. I bet that sand is scorching."

"Where's this place at?"

"A few miles down the road," he says, turning back around towards the living room. "We can either walk there or get a ride. Up to you."

"A walk sounds good," I say. "I haven't had a run in a few days, so I need the exercise."

"I didn't know you were a runner," he says. "Hadley is one, too. She drags me with her sometimes and I want to die."

"It's a nice way to clear my thoughts, I guess."

I get my wallet and my phone and make my way back to the kitchen.

"Ready to go?" he asks.

"Should I change first?"

"Will," he says, "you'd look good in dish rags. Let's go."

***

"How thick is it?" Elliot asks our waitress. She tilts her head and places her thumb and middle finger about an inch and a half apart.

"And how long you want it cooked matters too with that," she says.

"I like mine real thick," Elliot says, looking over at me.

I smile and look up at the waitress who is blushing now, trying to hide her need to laugh.

"I like mine real thick, too," she says, laughing.

"I'll have the same thing as him," I say, handing her my menu.

"Alright, you guys just hang tight while I go put this in for you."

"You just have a filthy mind today, don't you?

"I can't help it," he says. "I like my meat thick, what can I say."

"This is a pretty nice place," I say, looking around the room.

"Third time's a charm - hopefully."

Elliot unrolls his silverware from his napkin and puts them to the side and says, "So what's the plan for tomorrow?"

"I got an email before we left. I have to be at my meeting from nine till five."

"That's not too bad," he says.

"Nah," I say, taking a drink of my water. "I just hope you can find something to do while I'm gone."

"Don't worry," he says. "I'll find something or someone to do."

"Haha," I say. "You're too funny."

"I'll probably just sit on the beach and read all day to be honest. Work on darkening myself up. I love the exhaustion from being in the sun all day. It's weird."

"And then taking a nap once you get back in?" I say. "That would be the life: tan, eat, nap."

"Literally the life," he says, smiling.

Within the next half hour our food comes and Elliot's meat is thicker than he had hoped and he loves it.

"I never order steak," he says. "Honestly, I always go to a burger instead. This is delicious though."

"Thick enough?" I say, placing a piece in my mouth.

It really is delicious.

"I could handle something a little thicker, but yeah, it's sufficient."

I watch him as he takes each piece and places it in his mouth.

"What?" he says with food in his mouth.

"Nothing," I say. "Just watching you."

"Creeper," he says. "How's yours? Done enough?"

"It's perfect," I say. He looks back down at his plate and finishes off the rest of the meaty-parts on the steak.

Everything is perfect, I think to myself.

***

We get back to the hotel and sit down on the couch. The room is starting to get darker the later it gets and the sunset looks beautiful just from the living room window.

"Wanna watch a movie or something?" Elliot asks, grabbing the remote.

I sit my feet up on the table top and lay back against the couch.

"Whatever you want, stud," I say.

He flips it on a horror movie that I've never seen before and sets the remote back on the table.

He flips around and lays the length of the couch, sitting his legs on my lap.

"Do you mind?" he asks.

I set my left arm along the back of the couch and set my right palm on his leg, moving up and down from his ankle to his knee. His gaze is focused on the TV, but I see him smile as I rub back and forth.

"Do you like scary movies?" he asks.

"I love them," I say. "They don't exactly scare me, though."

"Yeah," he says, bringing his right arm behind his head. "Serial killers don't really match up to real-life fears. I mean neither is good, but at least killers disappear once defeated. Real things don't always disappear."

A woman screams on the movie and Elliot jolts a tad.

He looks up at me with his eyebrows raised and says, "It was a loud noise. Don't judge me."

I look over to my right and see my phone light up. It's Lydia.

***How's the trip?***

***Good. Watching a movie right now.***

I sit the phone back down on the counter. A minute later it lights up again.

***Good. Enjoy yourself. And be careful.***

I roll my eyes and sit the phone back down again.

"Not someone you want to talk to? Elliot asks.

"Just Lydia," I say.

"Making sure you're being careful?" he says, smiling.

"She just worries," I say. "I've had things happen in the past that make her on edge when I meet new men."

"Story for a later time?" he asks.

"Story for a later time," I nod. "I feel gross after being on that plane and in the sun. I'm gonna go shower real quick if that's OK?"

"I'll be here," he says, smiling up at me.

I make my way to the shower and close the door behind me.

As soon as the hot water touches my shoulder, I drift off into my own mind and I immediately start thinking about Elliot. I think back to the plane ride when he came up with his scenario about hot, passionate balcony sex.

Ever since I laid eyes on Elliot, I wondered what it would be like to have him - stretching my length inside of him and shoving myself deeper and deeper until I was apart of him.

I lather the washcloth with soap and wash my face. I slowly make my way down to my stomach and focus on Elliot again.

I picture him lying on the bed with his hands pressed against the mattress - back arched and ass pointed at a perfect angle for me to access. I lube myself up and stroke back and forth a few times to cover my full length.

I gently massage his hole with my thumb and palm both of his cheeks with my hands. I slowly stretch the muscles in and out, positioning myself over him. I rub myself up and down in between his cheeks and slowly force myself in. Elliot moans and I slowly pull out and push back in - stretching deeper and deeper every time I go back in.

He leans back and makes contact with my lips, positioning his right hand behind my head. I kiss his neck and speed up my thrusts, as he connects with my movements and slowly swings his ass in a circular motion.

I realize I've dropped the washcloth and see I'm beating the life out of my dick. I feel myself about to come and focus back on Elliot, as all energy quickly leaves my body and I have to position myself against the wall for balance.

I wash the rest of my body, rinse, and turn off the shower. I wrap the towel around my body and realize that I didn't bring any clean clothes into the bathroom with me.

I don't mind Elliot seeing me, but I don't want him to think I'm trying to lure him into the bedroom already.

I open the door and peek out into the living room, but he isn't on the couch anymore. I poke my head out into the living room and don't see him anywhere.

I make my way to my suitcase and notice a note made from the hotel pad.

***I'm on the balcony. Want to finish my story for me?***

# Chapter Seven

Elliot

THE SOUND OF THE WAVES crashing into the mainland clear my mind and I imagine each one making a pattern in the sand.

The air is cool and comfortable and I spread my feet farther apart and rest my arm on the railing.

If Will doesn't see my note before he comes out here then I'll feel like an idiot. Hopefully he doesn't think it's too rushed - even though it is. I think he wants me as much as I want him and I know I won't be able to sleep next to him tonight without rubbing one out at some point in the night.

I hear the sliding glass door softly screech open and then close and instantly get an anxious feeling in my gut

Is he going to say something? Should I turn around? Was this a bad idea?

I close my eyes and wait for him to do something. Seconds later, I feel his hands wrap around my stomach and my nipples instantly harden.

He presses his back into me and I can feel his cock press up against my back; it's rock solid. All I want to do is turn around and take him in my mouth, but I let things play out and he nuzzles his mouth into the right side of my neck.

I arch my head to the left and let out a soft moan as he kisses his way to my mouth.

He gently spins me around to face him and the moment my eyes lock with his, my cock hardens and I let out a heavy breath. He rubs the tip of his thumb under my bottom lip and pulls my mouth closer to his mouth, locking lips again. He makes his way down my neck and to my chest, taking each nipple in his mouth and gently biting them as he moves from one to the other.

He runs his hands down my stomach and gently palms my cock with his right hand while bringing his left one to my lips again for another kiss.

I run my hand down his chest and analyze the pattern his chest hair makes as I smooth my hand from his chest to his stomach. I run my hands down his stomach and take in each ridge as I move over his abdomen muscles.

His grip tightens on my cock and I let out a soft moan.

"I just showered and now you're gonna have me all filthy again," Will says, biting my bottom lip. "Also, this is nice and all, but it's getting a bit nippily out here."

"Agreed," I say, laughing.

"Come here," he says, picking me and wrapping my legs around his back. He turns around and I help him slide the door open.

He locks his mouth with mine again and he walks us to the bedroom - my dick bouncing around on his stomach as he switches feet and his dick gently skimming the middle of my ass cheeks as I bounce slightly.

He kneels down on the bed and pulls the covers back with his lips still locked with mine. He lays me back and runs his hands down my body, slowly making his way to my cock again. He grabs it again with his right hand and positions it right next to his lips. He licks the tip, never breaking eye contact with me, and slowly takes my full length in his mouth, moving up and down.

I arch my back with a moan, letting the pleasure of his mouth on me surge through every vein in my body. He looks up and gives a hint of a smile as he takes me deeper in his mouth.

I run my hands through his hair and start motioning my hips into the motion he has going. I feel myself starting to get close already and sit up because I don't want to come yet. He looks up confused at first, and then it registers and he smiles.

I lay him back on the bed and position myself over him. I make my way down his body, kissing his neck and then his chest. I kiss the different ridges of his stomach and then plant a kiss on the tip of cock.

I look up at him and see him bite his lip. His gaze focuses in on my lips and I make my way back down, taking his tip in my mouth. I can taste the body wash he used in the shower and I wonder if the rest of him tastes as good.

I take him deeper in my mouth and he moans, taking a fistful of my hair. He gently thrusts his hips forward and back in synch with my tongue along his length and I reposition myself over top of him, getting the best angle for his hips to move. I can feel his pulse vibrating through his cock and wonder if he is close or not.

He tilts my head up with his hand and brings it closer to his. His takes my tongue in his mouth and flips me onto my back on the bed again.

"I want you," I say. "All of you. Inside me." The words just come out and I don't even think about the fact that I've never asked a guy to shove himself inside of me before.

He smiles and gets off the bed, walking over to his bag. He pulls out a condom and a small bottle of lube.

"This probably looks bad," he says.

I get up off the bed and undo one of the pockets on my bag. I pull out a condom and a bottle of lube and say, "Same."

He laughs and walks over to me, setting the items on the nightstand next to the bed. He lies down on the bed and I take the condom wrapper and open it with my teeth. I roll the condom over his tip as he rubs the side of my hip softly. I gently squirt some lube over the tip and smooth it out over his whole length. He sits up and I position myself overtop of him. Slowly, I sit down edging him into me. After a few thrusts, he gets comfortably in and I push his chest back down.

I move my hips back and forth and I gently move up and down and he moans, lifting his knees slightly. I can feel him digging deeper and deeper into me, but I don't notice any sensation other than him poking against my prostate as he glides in and out.

He grabs hold of my cock and gently massages it back and forth, as I motion him in and out of me. The pleasure is unbelievable and I just want him deeper inside of me.

He readjusts his position and flips his position with mine, never coming out of me. He takes my hands and puts them behind my head against the wall and kisses my neck as he thrusts into me harder. He speeds up his thrusts and bites my bottom lip again.

I'm throbbing inside and with even the smallest touch, I might unload onto my chest.

"I'm close," he says, locking eyes with me. He locks his lips with mine again and slows down his thrusts. He shoves into me deeper and deeper the slower he gets and I can tell he is getting tired.

"You first," he says, pulling out of me and taking me in his mouth again. He shoves two fingers inside of me and continues to massage my prostate as he moves his tongue back and forth, all over my length. I can feel myself getting close and I let out a soft moan. He presses harder inside of me and goes down deeper on my cock.

"I'm coming," I say. "Com—"

I lean back and Will doesn't let up. I unload as he pounds at the tip of my cock. The pleasurable is unbelievable and I feel as though all the energy that I had in me is gone. He lets up and quickly shoves himself back inside me.

He lets out a loud moan and slowly his thrusts come to a halt. His breathing is heavy and he gives me a hint of a smile. He pulls out of me and leans his face down to mine. He softly kisses me and lies down next to me on the bed as he takes off the condom and ties it, throwing it in the wastebasket next to the nightstand.

"Pretty sure we did what your sister was telling you not to do with all that 'be safe' business," I say.

"Hey," he say, leaning on his side, "we were safe. We used protection."

"That's not what I meant," I say, laughing.

"I know," he says, smiling. "I can't help it. I've wanted that since we were in your car that night at the college."

"Satisfied?" I ask, leaning on my side as well.

"Beyond satisfied." He leans into me and kisses me on the lips again. "I'm hungry again," he says and gets up off the bed and goes into the bathroom.

"Wanna get pizza or something?" I ask him, getting off the bed and grabbing my phone.

"Yes, please."

I search on my phone for the best pizza places in town that deliver.

"What do you want on it?"

"I don't care," he says, wrapping his hands around my stomach and nuzzling his face into my neck. "Whatever you want."

"Yes," I say, trying to focus my attention on the person on the other line, "I just need a large pepperoni and cheese pizza and then an order of your breadsticks."

Will moves his hands from my stomach down to my cock and I let out a slight gasp. I look at him and smile and he raises his eyebrows.

"Delivery," I say, as he bites my shoulder and moves closer to my neck. I give the girl the address and room number and she rings up the total for me.

"Give us about a half hour to forty minutes," the girl says. I hang up the phone and turn around facing Will.

"A little over a half hour, probably," I say.

"Perfect," Will says smiling, and he pulls me back onto the bed.

***

The sunset has almost ran its course and it's getting harder and harder to see outside. Will and I both had a ridiculous amount of pizza and breadsticks and I feel like going and making myself vomit in the bathroom.

Sex with Will was good; sex with Will was grand. It didn't feel like it was rushed or that we had just hooked up. It felt real, raw and passionate.

"I'd like to retire here," I say, wiping my mouth with my napkin. "Have my morning coffee and read the paper like a regular retiree every morning when the sun rises."

Out of the corner of my eye I see my phone light up. It's Ethan.

***How goes it so far?***

***Good. Getting to know him a little more is nice.***

***How much of him have you gotten to know?***

***A good bit...***

***Was it good? I bet it was good. He is probably huge.***

***Goodnight, Ethan.***

"Ethan says hello," I say.

I see my screen light up again and this time it is Sam.

***Congrats, man. Ethan told me you finally got some. Jesus that was quick.***

***We went to the movies and he is staying over for the night.***

***I don't want him in my bed.***

***He's already made himself at home in it.***

***I'll call you tomorrow and give you the details.***

***OK. Tell Will I said hi and thanks for breaking my best friends yearlong sex hiatus.***

"Sam also says hi," I say, putting my phone back down on the table.

"Are they psychic or something?"

"No," I say, "just nosey."

"I'd like to retire here, too," he says. "A new book every few days and walks on the beach at night. Not alone though."

"I doubt you'll be alone."

"Let's hope not," he says, smiling. "I hope this thing tomorrow doesn't take too long."

"Just don't think about me," I say, laughing. "If you think about coming back and seeing me then it will probably drag."

"I can't ***not*** think about you, Elliot." His eyes focus on my lips and his face grows serious. "You're all I ever think about these days."

He gets up out of his chair and stands, leaning on the balcony railing.

He crosses his arms and says, "I was sitting in class the other day and a student had asked me a question and I was just lost in my own mind thinking about me and you here at the beach. Honestly, I don't know how I can want someone so much and barely know anything about him."

"What do you want to know?" I say, leaning on my elbow.

"Do you have any siblings?

"Only child," I say. "It always bothered me growing up because everyone I was friends with had that experience and I didn't."

"What made you want to be an editor?"

I get out of my chair and lean my arms on the balcony, facing the opposite way as Will.

"When I was younger," I start, "my parents used to fight a lot. Yelling, mostly, and sometimes stuff was thrown. It never got out of hand, but it was pretty constant. Most nights I would put earplugs in and sit down with a book. I visited the library constantly as a child and usually took two or three out at a time in case I finished one and needed another. Eventually, they got divorced and mom kept finding new guys to fight with."

He turns to his side and sets his hands down on the bar.

"Books were my escape I guess; from my reality to one where anything could happen. It's the only thing that ever interested me in school, so going to college was easy. Once I graduated, I left home and went to school in the city and never went back."

"Do you still talk to your parents?"

"Yeah," I say. "My parents loved me, I was never the issue. They just hated each other. They got divorced my sophomore year in high school and they visit me a good bit. Separately, of course."

I let out a deep breath and admire the sunset finally diminishing. There are families walking up from the beach, back to their hotels, and young couples walking in the sand taking pictures.

"It's made me hesitant about relationships to be honest. None of them have been successful."

"It's not because of that," Will says. "You have to have failed relationships before you find who you should be with."

"I gave up after my last one last year and focused on work"

Will leans off the balcony railing and says, "Sometimes you need that time to find yourself. It's when you reach that point that you no longer want anyone at all that is alarming.

We clean up all the trash from outside and put the extra pizza in the fridge. I sit down on the couch and Will lays down on me, this time with his head in my lap.

"If you don't mind me asking," he says, "what happened last year?"

"I don't know," I say. "It sounds dumb, because it is, but one day he came home and I could tell he had been crying and he said he couldn't do it anymore and was moving back home for a while to Indiana. He just up and left that night. I never got a text, phone call or reason in general for what was going on. It was just odd. Nothing led up to it either. It was just instant. Hadley told me the other night that he is back in town."

"Are you going to see him?"

"No," I say. "I have nothing to say to him really."

"Don't you want to know what happened?

"Yeah, I still do. If he wants to contact me he knows how."

I want to ask Will about his past and why it seems like such a touchy subject. I know he has something that he wants to tell me eventually, so I shouldn't force it out of him before he is ready. But I also really want to know.

"How long were you with him?" he says.

"Three years."

Will sits up and looks at me with raised eyebrows. "Three years and one day he just up and moves out because he can't do it anymore? There's more to that story, Elliot."

"It's a story that I ended last year," I say, grabbing his shoulder and bringing his head back down to my lap.

"Besides," I say, laughing, "if it hadn't happened then I wouldn't be here with you right now."

"But still I—"

"Do you want to watch a movie before bed?" I ask as smoothly as I can manage, trying to change the subject.

"I'll probably fall asleep right here," he says.

"That's fine with me," I say, running my hands through his hair.

Talking about Drew doesn't help the thought of moving on from him. He's no longer a subject that I care to talk about. It would've been different if we were madly in love, but we weren't.

We were both mostly done; being together just relived the sense of loneliness that we both were afraid to feel. I can't help but wonder why he really did leave that night, though.

I continue rubbing Will's head and try to focus on the waves crashing outside, as the thought of Drew escapes my mind and the thought of Will enters it.

# Chapter Eight

Will

ELLIOT LIES PEACEFULLY UNDER the covers, as I make my way to the bathroom and hop in the shower.

It's six in the morning and for the first time in a while, I feel completely refreshed from a night of sleep. Sex with Elliot was intoxicating. I've had sex plenty of times before, but never have I felt so comfortable so quickly with another guy like I did Elliot. And it wasn't weird after. I thought it would be challenging or that I wouldn't know what I was doing since it had been awhile, but with him, it was like we had been doing it for years.

The water hits my back and I lay my arm against the side of the shower and enjoy the change in my body temperature.

I'm pulled out of my daze when I hear the bathroom door creak open. I instantly feel my cock start to harden and lean off the wall as the sliding glass door of the shower starts to open. Elliot steps in and shuts the door, his expression focused.

"How much time do you have to spare?" he asks, grabbing the bottle of body wash sitting in the corner of the shower. He squirts some in his palm and rubs his hands together. He moves closer to me and puts both hands on my chest, rubbing them in circles.

"Plenty," I say, as he makes his way from my chest down to my stomach. He looks up at me, his hands never stopping their motions, and smiles as he moves his hands down form my stomach to my cock. He traces his thumb over the tip and I feel a surge of pleasure run through me and I harden.

"I want to take a ride this time," I say.

He sits back onto the seat that is in the shower and leans back onto his palms. He bites his lower lip as he looks my body up and down and I see his cock bounce back and forth as he situates himself on the seat. I lather up my palms and rub the soap on my backside and between my cheeks. I turn so my back is facing him and he palms a handful of my right cheek as he massages my middle with his left thumb.

He squirts a bit of body wash on his tip and rubs it over his whole length. He grabs each side of my waist and slowly pulls me back onto him. Slowly, I ease up and down, his cock sliding deeper into me each time I go down.

"Mmm," I hear him moan out as he tilts his head back and bites his bottom lip.

He leans up and kisses the different creases in my back, bringing his right hand to the base of my neck. I arch my body back as he brings my head closer to his and lock lips with him. His tongue finds every corner of my mouth and he brings his lips to my ear, biting on the lobe and tugging it gently.

He brings his hands around to my chest and my nipples harden at his touch. His right hand makes its way to my mouth and I suck on his thumb and pointer finger. His teeth graze my neck and I let out a moan as he forces his hips deeper into me, bouncing me gently.

I don't even notice the water hitting us both as I sway my hips up and down. He grasps my cock with his right hand and slowly jerks up and down, circling the tip with his thumb in each motion. The pleasure is unbelievable and I feel like coming already.

"I'm close," he says and I let out a sigh of pleasure.

"Me too," I say. I start to say his name as I arch my head back and unload all over his hand. He doesn't stop the motions with his hand and mercilessly massages the tip of my cock. He bites my ear and I feel like passing out from the pleasure of it all.

He lifts me off of him and, as he goes to stand up, I drop down to my knees, positioning my arms on his thighs and stick his cock in my mouth. He immediately leans his head back and moans. Seconds later, he unloads into my mouth and I don't let up, swirling my tongue around relentlessly until he drops from his elbows and lies back against the wall of the shower.

***

My conference lets out early and I race to the car to get back to the hotel. After the best shower of my life this morning, all I want to do is see Elliot and spend as much time with him as possible.

The drive takes about ten minutes and luckily there is a spot open right by the front doors of the hotel.

"Did you learn anything?" Elliot says as I walk in the door.

I loosen my tie and put my bag down on the kitchen counter. I make my way over to the couch where Elliot is laying down with one arm behind his head.

"Yeah," I say, lifting his feet and setting them on my lap as I sit down. "I learned the only thing more boring about a conference is a conference when you have a whole beach outside waiting for you."

"What do you want to do today?" he asks, smiling up at me. I look up from him to outside and then back down at him.

"I want to go get sand in my ass-crack."

"Same," he says, lifting his legs.

We make our way out of the hotel and walk the path to the sand right along where the waves are breaking. The sand is a cool temperature beneath my feet, but the sun is still smoldering against my skin as I sit my stuff down in the spot Elliot picks out.

"I've never been to the beach when it was so close to being fall," he says, spreading his towel on the ground.

He is wearing sky-blue swimming trunks that stop right above the knee and his shirt rides up his body as he leans down to even out the edges of his towel.

"I'm surprised by how hot it still is," he says.

"Really hot," I say, looking at his stomach as he takes his shirt off. I laugh and lie on my back. "Can we just stay right here forever?"

Elliot turns to his side and smiles at me.

"I'd love nothing more," he says. He switches onto his back and puts his hands over his eyes. "What do you want to do tonight?"

"I already have it planned out," I say.

"Oh really?" he asks. "More shower fun?"

"No," I say, laughing. "Well, maybe, but dinner first."

"Romantic."

"Just the Burger King around the corner," I say.

"No need to empty your bank account on little old me, Mr. Everett."

I switch to my stomach and lie on the right side of my face to look at Elliot.

"Should've brought a book or something," I say. "Isn't that what normal people do?"

"Yeah," he says, digging into the bag he brought down and pulling out a manuscript. "Most normal people do."

"You work while I take a nap," I say.

"Did you put lotion on?" he asks.

"No," I say. "Besides, I can't reach my back."

"I brought some down."

"I'm fine, Elliot."

"You're going to burn," he says, pulling out a highlighter from his bag.

"If I do," I start, "will you rub aloe on me?"

"Maybe," he says, flipping the page. "Just don't complain to me if it hurts. I'm not babying your ass."

"You look cute in those shorts," I say.

"I like even cuter out of them," he says.

We stay on the beach for a few hours and by the time we get up I am exhausted. The sun has dried me out and all I want to do is sleep.

"What time are we leaving here?" Elliot asks as he sits his bag down on the counter. The hotel room is chilly as the cool air hits my skin and I grow more tired as I make my way to the couch.

"After we take a nap," I say and he smiles at me.

"At least go sleep in the bed rather than the couch."

"I'm too tired," I say, frowning. "Carry me?"

Elliot walks over to the couch and lifts me onto his back. I wrap my arms around his neck and bury my face into his neck. His cologne sends a tingle through my body and I close my eyes as he lays me on my back on the bed.

I grab his arm and pull it towards me as he goes to get off the bed and he smiles.

"I thought you were tired?"

"I am," I say, dragging him to my left side, "but how am I supposed to sleep with you not cuddling me?"

He raises his eyebrow and rolls his eyes.

"One hour," I say. "Two hours tops."

***

Three hours later I wake up and it's dark outside.

"Refreshed?" Elliot says with his lips buried in my neck.

"How long have you been up?"

"One hour," he says. "Two tops."

"I'm sorry," I say, switching sides to look at him.

"I woke up awhile ago, but I wanted to let you sleep." His smile widens as I exhale a deep breath and he says, "What now?"

"Burger King," I say. "Or I thought we could go walk on the boardwalk a mile down the road and go eat at this little seafood place they have down there. Then lie along the beach and listen to the water. Star gaze and romantic shit like that."

He scrunches his face and takes a minute to think.

"Burger King is fine," he says.

"Shut up," I say, pulling him closer into me.

"I just want you to know, this has been one of the best weekends of my life. I'm beyond thankful that you sat down next to me that night on that park bench."

"Same," I say, bringing his face closer to mine and taking his bottom lip in my mouth.

I get off the bed and go brush my teeth in the bathroom. My hair is a mess and I can see where my skin has reddened from earlier. I squirt some gel in my palm and try to calm down the waves on my head.

"Looking a little red there," Elliot says behind me by the bed getting dressed.

I can see the edges and the definition of his muscles as he kneels and pulls up his pants. I focus back to myself in the mirror.

"Looks like your hands will be covered in aloe later," I say.

"Can't wait," he says, grabbing his toothbrush from the counter in the bathroom next to me.

"How is it you look fantastic when you wake up and I have to reorganize everything?" I ask him, staring at his bag-less eyes and perfectly maintained hair.

"Blessed I guess," he says, squirting toothpaste onto his toothbrush.

I make my way back to the bed and scrounge through my bag trying to decide what to wear.

"Jesus, Will," he says as I take my shirt off and throw it on the bed. I turn my back to the mirror and see it is beat red.

"It will be fine," I say.

"Until you wake up tomorrow and can barely move," he says.

"I'm tough," I say, flexing my arms to my sides and imitating a bodybuilder.

Elliot laughs and rinses the rest of the bubbles from his mouth. He dries his mouth on the towel and makes his way to the bed and says, "I don't know what to wear."

He looks through my bag and pulls out a light blue button up and the cream colored shorts I brought with me.

"Done," he says, smiling up at me. I take off my pants and his eyes shift from my face down to my crotch. I slowly pull on my shorts and his smile widens.

"Trying to torture me?" he asks as I button my shorts.

"Maybe," I say, bringing the shirt behind my back. I can feel it gently brush against my back and from how cool it feels, I can tell how hot my back must feel right now from the sun. I button the shirt up all the way and put my arms out.

"Good?" I ask.

He raises his eyebrows at me and gets off the bed. He stands in front of me and unbuttons one more button on my shirt, exposing some chest hair.

"I always feel like a douche without having it buttoned up to the collar."

"I like it," he says, turning around and going out to the kitchen. "The chest hair is nice."

"What if other people think it's nice tonight?"

"I hope they do," he says. "Let them look. It doesn't matter because I'm the one who gets to go back home and lay my head against it at the end of the night."

***

We get to the boardwalk and there are just enough people that we aren't shoulder to shoulder.

"Over there," I say, pointing to the restaurant that sits out over the ocean along the boardwalk.

It's a completely open, shack looking area and they have multicolored lights overhead of each booth. We make our way to the bar area and take a seat.

"What can I get you guys?" the bartender says, drying out a shot glass. She smiles once she sees us and her eyes wander to my collar. I try to contain my smile while Elliot bumps my shoulder.

"Can we order food right here too or just drinks?" Elliot asks her.

She pulls two menus out from under the counter and lays them in front of us.

"All of it is fresh," she says. "Fish and chips is our most popular thing that people get. Pretty damn good, too." Her eyes wander from me to Elliot and her smile never wavers. "My name is Stephanie, by the way, and once you guys know what you want just let me know and I'll send the order downstairs."

"I was wondering where the food came from," I say.

"Yeah, the stairway is hidden on the other side of the bar. Most people don't even know it's there honestly."

"I'll just take a water for now," I say.

"Same," Elliot says, looking down at his menu. "Some wine once the food is out."

Elliot smiles up at her and she blushes and she fills two glasses with water.

"Are you two on vacation?" she asks, sitting the glasses down.

"Wor—"

"Honeymoon," Elliot says, before I can get out the word.

Her smile widens and she says, "I knew you two were way too pretty to be straight. You guys are gorgeous together."

"Oh, he's the gorgeous one," he says, running his fingers through my hair. "I figured he would make beautiful children, so I said why not."

She laughs and looks over at me and says, "And you wanted to be with a comedian I'm guessing?"

"I love a sense of humor," I say, looking over at him smiling. "We'll just take the fish and chips I think."

"I'll be right back," she says as I hand her the menus.

"Really?" I say, grinning.

"Free drinks, William." He takes sip of his water and laughs and says, "Told ya people love that extra button. She probably would've gone home with you if you'd asked her."

"She probably still would," I say.

"Ew," he says, shaking his head. "I don't like to share. How's your back feel?"

"I can feel the heat radiating off it, but it's fine."

He puts his hand on my back and gently rubs up and down the crease of my spine.

"Maybe next time you'll listen to me, yeah?"

"Doubt it," I say.

I look over to my right and see a drink list lying on one of the stools. I grab it and set it in front of the both of us and say, "What wine goes with fish?"

"I don't want wine," he says. "I don't know why those words even came from my mouth to be honest. The house beer looks good here."

I look up and to my right at the bar across from us and freeze. The guy sitting there, talking to the woman next to him, looks exactly like Evan and I start struggling to breathe. I can't believe this is happening right here and now.

"Will," Elliot says, touching my shoulder. "What's wrong? Will look at me."

I look over to Elliot and then back over to the guy at the bar. My head is clearer and I can tell now it isn't him. I look back over to Elliot and am at a loss for words.

"Sorry," I say, laying my elbows down on the counter.

"What was that?"

"It's nothing," I say, shrugging. "I'm fine."

"It looked like you were having a panic attack and unless I'm making you super fucking nervous, I'm not sure what exactly would have caused it."

"It just happens sometimes," I say, taking a drink of water.

I look over at him and he looks away. I look back to the guy at the bar and see that they have left.

"I get it," he says. I look back over at him and he locks his hands together on the table. "Not there yet. You can tell me when you're ready."

"I'm sorry," I say again.

He looks over at me and manages a smile. He puts his hand on my back again and moves it back and worth.

"It's fine," he says.

Stephanie comes out seconds later with our food and Elliot tells her thank you for the both of us. The silence is deafening between us and I don't know what to do.

"It's PTSD," I say, bringing a piece of fish to my mouth. Out of the corner of my eye I see him turn towards me, but I look straight ahead and down at my food. "My ex isn't really an ex. He died last spring."

Elliot's face grows more serious, but he shows no sign of emotion - still focused.

"How long were you guys together?" he asks.

"Four years," I say, taking a drink of water.

To our right, fireworks go off over the ocean. The sky fills with blues and reds and greens and everyone around the bar area turns to look at them. I turn towards Elliot and his gaze hasn't wavered from my face.

"He was in a bad car accident last year. He was—"

"How does your guys' food taste?" Stephanie says, cutting me off. A wave of relief comes over me and I turn back to my food.

"It's great," Elliot tells her, grinning from ear to ear.

Stephanie walks to the other side of the bar and Elliot scoots forward on his bar stool.

"We don't have to talk about it right now," he says. "Let's change the subject. What all do you have to do tomorrow at your thing?"

"Present again. Early in the morning, though, so once I do we can get going. Our flight isn't till two, though, so we still have time to eat and shop or whatever."

"I still mean what I said," he says, finishing off the last of his fries. "This really has been a great weekend. I just want you to know that."

***

The sand is cool running through my fingers as we lie down outside our hotel. The moon is bright and all I can hear is the sound of the waves crashing in the distant.

"I wish I could stay in this moment," Elliot says. "Here with you on this blanket, the moon radiating off the water. It's great and peaceful."

"I'm sorry," I say.

"Will—"

"No," I say. "I'm sorry for earlier. And I'm sorry that it's so hard for me to explain it to you."

"I knew you had something that you were hiding," he says. "Days ago we were talking and you got awkward at a point over something I don't remember, but right then I wondered what it was that clicked in your brain. You don't owe me an explanation anyway. It's only been a few weeks of knowing each other."

"It doesn't seem like it, though," I say.

"I know," he says, "but it has been, so it's fine. You can tell me when you are more comfortable."

"Thanks for coming on this trip with me," I say.

"Thanks for asking me to come."

I move my head onto Elliot's chest and he wraps his arm around me. I feel safe and comfortable in his arms, in this moment. I look up to the moon and realize that everything might be OK and that happiness is still out there for me to find.

I can't help but think about Evan, though, and the sense of betrayal I feel for being here with Elliot.

# Chapter Nine

## Elliot

IT'S ALMOST TEN O'CLOCK and our check out for the hotel is at eleven. Will had me drop him off so I could have the car to leave in case he wasn't out in time.

He was anxious this morning and I know it's because of what happened last night at the pier. My reassurance won't fix anything, so I'll just have to wait it out and hope he doesn't worry about it the whole way home. Something bad must have happened to have him this affected by it. But I'm not going to worry about it.

I check one last time to make sure I didn't leave anything behind. I grab both of our bags and head out the door.

"Did you have a pleasant stay?" the girl behind the counter asks. She looks bored and her forced smile is causing her pain I'm guessing.

"It was super," I say without grinning back. "Thanks."

I make my way to the car and set the bags in the backseat. I check my face in the mirror and can see my skin has a tint of red. It isn't, however, burnt like Will's who got out of bed this morning rigid and tight like a piece of leather.

When I pull up to the curb outside of the building, Will is talking to some woman and shaking her hand as he walks away toward me. He opens the door and lets out a large exhale.

"Long morning?"

He turns to me and smiles and says, "That woman was one of the coordinators of the whole thing and she was asking me questions about Chicago and their education system as far as the suburban areas. Can we go eat?"

***

We get sat at the Italian restaurant beside a bubbly, heavy-set redhead who has worked at the airport for over five years and absolutely loves everything the area has to offer.

"It's nice," Will says. "I couldn't live here, though. Way too hot."

"How long are you guys in for?" she asks.

"Our flight leaves at two, actually," he says.

"Well this was a good stop before heading out at least."

"What do you recommend?" I say, holding up the menu.

She gets out of her chair and comes over and stands over my shoulder.

"This platter has a bunch of random stuff," she says, pointing down to my menu. "Should fill you boys up."

"Marcia," the guy at her table says, getting out of his seat, "let's go."

"It was nice meeting you boys," Marcia says, touching Will's shoulder on the way towards the exit. Her husband looks back once she is in front of him and mouths 'sorry'. I wave him off and smile and look over to Will who is zoned into his menu.

"She was nice," I say, bringing him out of his daze.

"Quite the character that one," he says. "This platter does look really good."

"Then it's a done deal." I take a sip of my water and lay my menu down on top of his.

"How's your sunburn?"

"I should have listened to you," he says, putting his hands in his face. "It feels terrible."

"At least you'll be nice and tan this Fall."

"Are you still going to aloe me up?"

"Absolutely."

He smiles and looks down to his hands. A frown grows across his face and he scrunches his eyebrows and I say, "What's wrong? Is this still about last night?"

"No," he says, "sorry."

"Then what is it?"

"I don't enjoy teaching anymore." He leans his head back and lets out a sigh. "I realized that this morning after presenting. I know bringing this up right now is stupid, but it's bugging me."

He looks up at me and forces a small smile.

"Let's run away together," I say. "Live in the woods and just have hot gay sex all day."

"My thoughts exactly," he says, laughing. "Thank you."

"For what?"

"This weekend," he says. "Not freaking out last night. Being a good guy."

"It's all an act."

"Well," he says, "it's a good one that I'm enjoying being a part of."

"Hey guys, I'm Walter and I'll be your waiter on this beautiful Sunday afternoon." Walter is a smallish, older man with the most adorable smile and sharpest looking outfit I've ever seen on someone for his age. "I see she got you guys your drinks. Are you ready to order or still need some time?"

"We're gonna have this Italian platter thing," Will says, pointing to his menu.

"Alright," Walter says, picking up our menus. "You guys sit tight."

"So," I say, leaning back in my chair, "if you don't want to teach then what do you have in mind?"

"I really like helping people," he says. "Going overseas years ago was the best thing I had ever done. I saw what it meant to the kids and there wasn't a moment where I wasn't happy doing what I was doing. I need something like that again; something fulfilling and meaningful. I need something where I have no doubt that I'm making a difference."

"Run an organization. With all your experience I'm sure you could find the backers and do something life changing."

"I'll look more into it when we get back," he says. "That or maybe I should just not teach college in general. I could always step down to something else.

He takes a drink of water and a huge grin shines across his face from ear to ear.

"What?" I ask, smiling.

"I'm just thinking about things," he says. "Specifically this morning before I left."

I situate my legs as I feel my pants stiffen. The thought of Will's mouth all over my cock makes me want to take him in the bathroom here and now. He notices me switch positions and lets out a laugh.

"I'm glad you think me being hard right now is so funny," I say, laughing.

"I find it flattering."

"We have had a lot of sex this weekend," I say. "Not that I'm complaining, but I'm pretty wore out."

"Guess the job is getting done then."

"Done very, very well," I say.

***

We eat our food and make our way to the airport. We drop the car off at the rental facility next door and walk the rest of the way to the entrance doors.

We sit down to wait it out until our flight leaves and my leg is anxiously moving up and down.

"Chill," Will says, putting his hand on my knee. "It will be fine."

"I know," I say, swinging my head back. "But you never know."

"What time are you guys having dinner tonight?"

"Around seven," I say, taking out my phone and confirming the text from Ethan. "It's going to be exhausting."

"Why?" Will asks with a laugh.

"They're all nosey as hell. They mean well, but they'll badger me until I tell them everything I did."

"All three of them seem amazing. Well, I haven't really met Ethan yet."

"Maybe us three can have dinner this week," I say.

"Yes please," he says.

Minutes go by and they finally announce our flight is boarding. Will is more quiet than usual and I'm sure it is because of last night.

"Are you OK?" I ask him as I sit down from putting my carry-on in the overhead storage.

His eyes shift from the window to me and he shifts his body toward me all together.

"I still feel weird about last night," he says, looking down at my hands and back up to my face.

"I told you it's fine," I say.

"No," he says, "it isn't."

I grab his hand and cup it between mine and say, "Will, we've only known each other a few weeks. I'm perfectly fine with getting to know you little by little, more and more each day. With that, I don't have to know every single thing immediately. I'm patient."

"Just tell me when you're ready," I say. "Once you're comfortable enough with me and can handle saying it."

"Okay," he says with a smile.

***

"So, twelve inches, right?" Ethan spits out while practically deep-throating his fish sandwich.

Sam couldn't make it because he had a last-minute meeting with a client about finalizations on a book cover that he designed so I have the pleasure of the Alexander-twins.

"I can't believe you had sex with him already," Hadley mumbles just loud enough for me to catch every word.

"I couldn't help it," I say, laughing. "The worst thing with someone is sexual-tension."

"But you've only known him for a few weeks and it's not like he is a random hook-up for you," she says. I look from her to my food and she puts her fork down. "All I'm saying is every relationship that I have had where I had sex with the guy in less than four weeks has never worked out for me."

"You also prefer sleeping with your gun compared to a person," Ethan says, sitting his fork down to catch his breathe. "I think it's awesome, El. I wouldn't have been able to make it past week one."

"Speaking of, how's Paul?" Hadley says, resting her chin on her cupped hands.

"I don't know," Elliot says with a mouthful of fries. He leans back in his chair and folds his arms behind his head.

He swallows and says, "He's a good lay, but he really is stupid. God wasn't thinking when he made something that beautiful yet so dumb." He sits straight again and focuses back on his food. "I think I want more to be honest."

I look at Hadley and I can feel a spaghetti noodle fall right out of my mouth just as her mouth slowly widens as well.

"Like a relationship or just a smarter person?" I ask him.

"Both," he says.

"What?" he says, as we both look from each other to him.

"Just weird to here you say is all," Hadley says with a laugh.

Ethan looks over at me and his face is serious.

"What's wrong?" I ask him.

"I just think it's time I move on from everything that happened. It's been awhile and I need to move on from it."

"You can't force the healing of that, though," Hadley says.

"But I at least need to try," he says.

His eyes start to moisten and for the first time in years, I see Ethan drop to a new level of vulnerability that he isn't used to being in.

"Sorry," he says. "I just made things awkward for no reason."

He pushes his plate to the side and crosses one leg over the other, leaning on the table. "So, back to William."

"What about him?" I say, laughing.

"What all did you guys do?" Hadley asks me. "Besides sex."

I take a minute to think about what I want to say because the first thought that enters my mind is Will's breakdown at dinner. Most people don't start relationships off with random and awkward events like the one we had and I'm not sure how they will react to it.

But it doesn't matter what they think.

"It was great," I say. "Last night was different, though."

Hadley raises her eyebrows and Ethan looks over to the bar-area at a group of suited gentleman who are either playing dress-up or had a late Sunday meeting.

"I think Will has a past that he isn't ready to tell me about yet."

"I could do some digging on him," Hadley says, eyes focusing in on my every word.

"No," I say. "I mean, it's not like he used to do drugs or was an alcoholic or killed someone kind of past. It's about his ex."

Ethan reverts his attention back to me and rests his head on his left hand.

"Still isn't over him?" he asks.

"He died," I say. I see Hadley shift in her seat and a hint of a frown grows over her face. Ethan looks down at the table and then looks back up to me. "A car accident I guess. He was getting into telling me, but the waitress there interrupted him before he could get it all out and I could see he was feeling nervous about it."

"I mean," Hadley starts, "this just randomly came up or what?"

"He had a panic attack while we were eating."

Ethan laughs and I look up at him.

"I'm sorry," he says, stopping himself, "really, that isn't funny, but it's just surprising that's all."

"That he has panic attacks?"

"I see people like Will who are extremely beautiful and are well-off career-wise and then you find out that they aren't perfect and have feelings and such and it just confuses me."

"You are beautiful and well-off career-wise and you are one of the most damaged people I have the privilege of knowing," I say with a smile.

"Touché," he says.

"So you didn't talk about it after that?" Hadley asks.

"No," I say, "and that's OK. I mean, we've only known each other a few weeks so I still have things to learn about him. A lot of things."

Hadley looks at me and her face slowly morphs into a high-dimpled grin.

"What?" I say, twirling the spaghetti around on my fork.

"I just haven't seen you this invested in awhile, and I like it."

"It's still early," I say.

"But you like him," she says. "You like him a lot. And I like him too, so that's a plus."

"He's just different," I say. "The comfort I feel with him is different than what I'm used to and I feel safe in his presence I guess." I brush my fingers along the rim of my glass and feel the moisture suction into my pores. "I never felt like that with Drew. I mean, even in the early stages with him I never felt like I needed to be around him all that much. He was just a part of my life."

"Maybe that's why you weren't as broken up when he left as you could've been," Hadley says.

I look over at her and she pushes her plate to the side. The waitress brings over the checks and sits them down beside Hadley.

"I think you only cared so much when he left because of the way he did and not because you didn't know how your life without him in it was going to be," she says, handing me my bill. "I liked Drew, but I never understood it. You never looked at Drew the way I saw you look at Will that night at dinner."

"I don't look at Will any different," I say, laughing.

"Yes, you do," she says, smiling. "It's almost child-like. You look at him in a way that I can only dream to look at someone one day."

"Well if you would—"

"Shut up, Ethan," Hadley says, throwing him his bill.

"When am I going to get the pleasure of properly meeting your boyfriend?" Ethan says.

"I told him maybe we could all do dinner this week sometime."

"What about Friday and then I can drink too and really welcome him into our club?"

"Or you could not drink a lot and relax and remember meeting him the next day," I say.

"Fine," hc says, signing his signature on his receipt. "Does he have any gay friends he can bring along?"

"I'll ask him," I say.

"Or a gay brother would be nice, too."

"He doesn't have one, bud."

"Well, what the fuck. That's not fair."

"I know. The world is unfair sometimes."

"Extremely," he says.

***

"So, Friday?" I ask Will while washing the dishes from dinner the following night.

"What about it?"

"Are you busy?"

"Nope," he says, grabbing my waist from behind. "Why, what's up?"

He rests his chin on my shoulder and I can feel the tiny hairs from his beard prickling into my skin through my shirt.

"Dinner with my crew."

"Your crew," he says, laughing. "That sounds enticing."

"I already basically set it up, so if you don't go then you'll look like a dick," I say, rubbing the side of my head against his.

"Well then I have no choice," he says, kissing my cheek.

Will walks back to the living room and sits down on the couch. The couch is black leather and makes a very small squeak when he sits down and I smile.

The counter tops in the kitchen are gray-marble and the cabinets are all a bright shade of white that gleam under the light.

My apartment still has the same things it had when I moved in years ago because I could care less, so being in Will's makes me realize how little effort I've put in to making a home for myself where I live.

"How long have you been at this place?" I ask him, rinsing the last dish and putting it to the side.

"A little over a year," he says.

I walk over to the couch and lay my head on his lap towards the TV.

"It's really nice," I say. "Way better than my place."

"I hate renting," he says. "I just haven't really found a place I'd like to settle down in yet, though, as far as houses."

"The thought of owning a house alone depresses me," I say, moving my vision to his face.

He leans down and locks me in for a kiss, his hands on both sides of my face.

"Same," he says.

"You're cute."

"I know," he says.

"Have you seen your sister since you've been back?" I ask him, stealing the remote.

"Going over Thursday," he says.

He runs his fingers through my hair and I close my eyes, imagining the two of us back by the beach, away from real life. Visions of the sun setting, Will's head on my chest in the middle of the night and our bodies together that last night on the beach all cross my mind and I smile.

Will flips the channel and I hear shooting and a cop siren. My mind slowly goes to dinner that last night and his breakdown and the exhaustion on his face when he came out of it.

I shift off his lap and sit up rubbing my right eye.

"What's wrong?" he says, confused.

I look at the TV and squint.

"Nothing," I say, moving closer into him.

"Are you sure?"

I don't want to bring it up because I told him I was patient and I am. It has bugged me ever since, though, because it affected him so much and I don't know how to act with him about it. I turn my body towards him and bite my cheek in thought.

"What, Elliot?"

"I'm sorry," I say with a small laugh. "I just can't stop thinking about Saturday night."

His face tightens and his skin starts to redden.

"I know," he says.

He leans his head on his hand, his elbow resting in a dip on the side of the couch. He runs his fingers through his hair with his other hand and scratches his scalp.

"I'm sorry," I say, moving in my seat. "This is rude of me."

"No," he says ,putting his hand on my shoulder. "It's OK."

He turns and faces me. I watch his chest slowly rise and fall as he, I imagine, attempts to calm his nerves.

"I was living in a house with Evan at the time. We had bought it about six months before the accident." He locks eyes with me and then quickly looks away. "Evan was on his way back from Indiana visiting his mom. It was late and I knew he would get home after I had fallen asleep. I was tired and fell asleep on the couch with my phone by my head when I got the call from his mom."

His eyes start to moisten and I sit my hands in his lap. He grabs them, enclosing them in his own and forces a small smile.

"He was about a half-hour outside of the city and a drunk driver had hit him head on."

"I'm sorry, Will." I pull him in closer and he leans his head on my shoulder.

"That isn't the worst part of it all," he says with a slight sob. He goes silent and his breathing slows down. I stiffen and slowly run my fingers through his hair.

"I got to the hospital just as they were bringing him in off the stretcher and I couldn't even recognize him. He was screaming and—"

"It's OK," I say, lifting his face up to mine. "You don't have to go into detail about it. You don't have to relive it."

He sits up, takes a deep breath, and wipes his eyes with his thumb and pointer-finger.

"It's why I have my attacks. It's why I ***used*** to have my attacks at least. I'd think about it before going to bed or if I saw his family. For the longest time, I couldn't picture the real him. All I could see was the version of him after the wreck and it was like experiencing a non-stop nightmare in my mind."

"What helped you?"

"A therapist," he says. "Went to a few meetings regarding loss. Not seeing his family helped, but that wasn't fair to them. Basically I just tried to move on as best I could."

"It might've been easier if you hadn't done it alone," I say.

"I know," he says, turning his gaze towards me. "I saw his sister weeks ago at the store and it triggered it again. Just seeing her face made me see things I didn't want to and I had to leave the store."

I look from his eyes to his lips and then down to the floor.

He laughs and says, "I'm sure now I look like a relationship is the last thing I need."

I move closer to him and lie between his legs, saddling up to his chest. I wrap his arms around me and say, "I think it may be exactly what you need." He bends down, kisses the top of my forehead and lays his chin on my head.

I pull the throw blanket from the top of the couch and lay it over us, inhaling the scent of Will, and think about the comfort I feel in his arms. Weeks seem like months with Will and I don't know whether to love that feeling or be afraid of it. What I do know is he opened up to me tonight and it brought us closer than we both probably realize in this moment.

# Chapter Ten

Will

"I'M JUST SURPRISED YOU told him already is all," Lydia says, setting Abbey's grilled cheese on the coffee table.

Abbey tears a piece off, forces it into her mouth with four fingers and then focuses her attention back to the TV where an animated cat and her dog friend are trying to find their squirrel friend.

Apparently, the dog says something funny in the mind of a two-year old and Abbey breaks out into giggles and looks over at me with a smile.

"It was bothering him not knowing."

"And that's a good reason to tell him? Because he was impatient?"

"No," I say. "He was being patient and he still would've been. It's better that I got it out."

Lydia sits down in the chair opposite the couch where Abbey and I are and crosses one leg over the other.

"Well," she says, "you seem happy today at least. Maybe relieved?"

"I just don't know if what I need right now is another relationship."

"Maybe that's exactly what you need."

"That's what Elliot said," I say.

Lydia laughs and says, "Well maybe we are right. Just because you haven't completely healed doesn't mean that there isn't room for someone new in your life. I think Elliot could help you heal the rest of the way."

"You don't even know him."

"Yeah," she says, folding her arms across her chest. "I know I don't. Let's change that."

"What?"

"I want you to invite him to breakfast with us on Sunday. I'll be able to tell pretty quick if he is right for you or not and then if I don't like him, you don't have to date him."

I roll my eyes at her and make my way to the kitchen. I get a glass of water and refill Abbey's cup of juice and make my way back to the couch.

"I'll ask him," I say, taking a drink.

"So, dinner with his friends tomorrow, huh?"

"I've met the two," I say, sitting the glass down on the table. "I just have to meet the last one."

"What about his family?"

"They don't live in the city. And he's an only child."

"Well that's no fun," she says.

"Yes," I say, crossing my arms over my chest, "he will never know the sheer joy of having someone bully him at a young age or questioning the decisions he makes in his adult life."

***

"Will, this is Ethan," Elliot says as we go to sit down.

I smile and Ethan beams back. He ignores my handshake and embraces me for a hug that is a little tighter than expected.

"You smell amazing," Ethan says as he lets go and I laugh.

"Really?" Elliot says to Ethan as I scoot into the booth next to Hadley.

Hadley leans into my ear and says, "He's really not that weird. He just likes to make a very odd first impression with new people so you know what you are getting into." I laugh and look over at Ethan who is already checking out someone at the bar-area.

"Did you guys hear about that old man getting shot a couple blocks from here Wednesday night?" Sam asks, looking around the table. He looks at Hadley and raises his eyebrows in a well-you-must-have way.

"Samuel," she says, crossing her arms over her chest, "do you realize how many people get shot in Chicago on an hourly, even minutely, basis let alone a daily basis? I don't know every crime that happens and I don't even work in this part of the city." She lifts her menu off the table and flips the page.

"But yes," she says with a smile, "I did hear about it."

"Okay," Sam says. "Well, it turns out that old guy was the husband to that woman I was talking about the other day who's hobby is spending all her husband's riches and writing shitty books about vampires and such. She called me earlier today to tell me about the fact and said that she appreciated all I had done, but the one cover was going to be all that she did because she didn't have the time to finish her series now."

"Whatever will we do," Elliot says.

"I know," Sam says with a frown. "I just couldn't believe it was her husband. I wonder if she hired someone to do it. She didn't sound too concerned about the fact on the phone."

"Well I wouldn't be either if I was a gold-digging whore who just gained access to my husbands fortunes," Hadley says, raising her eyebrows.

"So, Will," Ethan says, focusing his attention back on myself and the group, "you're a professor?"

"Yep," I say. "A few years now. Don't know how much longer, though."

"What else do you see yourself doing?"

"I don't know," I say. I take a pause and say, "I know I like helping people and teaching them things, but I don't think the college setting is the place I should be doing it."

"I know of a lot of youth organizations and stuff like that that could use some guidance and help in general," Hadley says. "One in particular that I know of has been trying to get funding for a while now and I heard the other day that things are finally starting to look up. It's for young, LGBTQ youths and some of the funding is actually contributed from the police department because they are trying to get more involved and show that they are accepting and things like that."

"Anything to save face," Elliot says.

"Basically," she says with a nod. "I'll find out more about it and let you know."

"Second time seeing Hadley and she already has you a new job," Elliot says, rubbing my back.

"I know," I say as the waiter comes over to our table. "Your friends are amazing."

"You're lucky," Ethan says, closing his menu up. "She can be a real bitch sometimes."

Hadley throws her straw-wrapper at him and we all try to order in spite of the laughter we can't contain.

"Elliot told me the other day that you have been looking into other things is all," she says. "This opportunity would be great for you, though."

***

Two hours, baskets of fries, pounds of meat, and several beers later, Ethan is telling us all the story of how last night he broke up with the guy who he has been seeing named Paul, but not before he had sex with him one last time.

"You couldn't just *walk* away could you, bud?" Elliot says, digging his face into my shoulder and trying to keep from falling over from laugher. I'd never seen Elliot with this much alcohol in him, but he is ridiculously happy and I love every single minute of it.

"You do smell good, William," Elliot says, sniffing my neck. He plants a kiss on my cheek and turns his focus back to Ethan.

Taking a swig of his beer, he says, "What did he say before you actually did leave?"

"He was asleep," Ethan says with wide eyes. "I wore him out with our last sha-bonga and I slipped out before he could wake up and remember it and stuff and yeah I just left because why not and I haven't heard from him and that's good because yeah and he needs to find someone else or something else like a dictionary because he's stupid."

Ethan finishes off his beer and sits it on the side. He picks up one of his leftover fries and holds it inches from his face. He finally eats it and says, "Cock of gold, though. Cock of gold."

"They never usually drink this much," Sam says to my right, having taken Hadley's spot who had to leave early because of work again. "Well, Elliot never does at least."

I look over at Elliot and he is focused in on Ethan who is telling him a new story about this bar he installed security at a few days before. I can tell he is getting tired because he is slowly moving from side to side and his eyelids are getting closer together.

"I like how free he is when he drinks," I say. "He's that way when he doesn't drink, too. I'm the opposite. I'm an emotional mess I feel like."

"Me too," Sam says, laughing. "I never drink if I'm dating someone because by the end of the night, I've either planned our wedding or accused them of cheating on me and it always ends with them thinking I'm crazy."

"Elliot hasn't mentioned if you were with anyone," I say, wiping my hands on my napkin and throwing it on my plate.

"I was," he says. "A few months ago I was still with my ex, Andrew, and he actually had been cheating on me for two out of the three years that we were together."

I raise my eyebrows and he laughs and says, "I came home early one day and found him screwing the neighbor on the dining room table."

"Like the Andrew that you guys work for?"

"No," he says. "No, no. Different guy. Same level of douchebag-ness, though."

"That sucks, man."

"It wasn't my table, so I didn't get as upset as I could have."

I laugh and he takes a drink of his tea.

"I moved out the next day and Elliot had his spare room, so I just moved on in and ever since have made it a point to tell everyone Andrew knows that he is a cheating, cock-sucking asshole who will die alone."

"Have you went out with anybody since or just focusing on yourself right now?"

"Focusing on myself," he says, nodding. "I don't know. I love being in a relationship and having someone to come home to at night, but to be honest, I've always been with someone and I'm kind of enjoying my time alone right now. Focusing on work."

Sam nods towards Elliot and I make a quick glance over at him and then back to Sam.

"He was focusing on work, too, before you came into the picture; in a different way. For the wrong reasons."

"He told me his ex left," I say.

"Yeah," he says. "He pretends like it didn't bother him that much, but I know it did. But I will say the way he looks at you and the way he acts around you and even the way he talks about you, he *never* was that way with Drew. Drew was just someone to spend time with and be with so he didn't have to be alone. Drew was his comfort-zone."

Sam coughs, lets out a small laugh and says, "I'm sorry. Some real-talk just felt the need to relish from my body I guess."

"It's OK," I say. "Real-talk is better than random babble."

"But seriously," he says, moving closer to me, "I know it is early for you two, but you're helping Elliot in ways that I don't think he realizes yet."

I look over at Elliot and catch him mid-laugh in a conversation with Ethan. He brings his hand to his mouth to keep himself from spitting out his drink and Ethan has his head lying on the table, dying from laughter. In this moment, all my worries about my career are gone. All I see is Elliot and a chance at a happiness I had lost over a year ago when Evan was taken away from me. I see myself healing and slowly, all the darkness that has clouded my mind seems to be diminishing.

***

I wake up Saturday morning to the sound of Elliot dry-heaving on the floor of my bathroom. It's seven in the morning and while I feel fantastic, I look from my bed, straight into the bathroom, and see his hands folded on top of the toilet seat and his hair slicked back from sweat.

I get up and slowly make my way to the bathroom. I lean against the side of the doorframe and smile. He looks up at me and his eyes are filled with moisture - his face stern and serious.

"I've been here all night," he says and looks back to the bottom of the toilet bowl.

I grab a washcloth underneath the sink and wet it with warm water. I wring it out and sit down next to Elliot. Even with the faint smell of vomit surrounding him and sweat drenching every part of his head and upper-body, I can't help but relish in the fact that this beautiful man is in my life.

I move behind him and gently lean him back into my chest. I lift the washcloth and wipe away the sweat above his brow and along his forehead. He takes my left hand and cups it between his, sitting it on his thigh.

"Thank you," he says with exhaustion. "I never drink that much. Not since college."

"I know," I say. "How about you shower and I'll get you some water?"

"How about I just curl myself around your toilet and stay here until tomorrow?"

I reach over and turn the shower on – making sure the water is cool rather than warm.

"Come on," I say slowly helping him onto his feet. He sits on the side of the bathtub and I help him with his socks and pants. He takes off his shirt and hands it to me as he slowly turns his body into the tub and sits down inside it.

"The water is on the other—"

"I know, William," he says, sighing. He lifts the shower curtain up and over his head and disappears to the other side.

As I make my way to leave the bathroom, I hear the shower curtain slightly open and see his head popped out.

"Thank you," he says and slowly closes it back up. I smile and throw his clothes on the floor next to the washer and dryer.

Twenty minutes later, I look down the hallway and see Elliot walk from the bathroom into the bedroom. I grab a large bowl and grab his glass of water and make my way to the bedroom.

"Did you have anything special to do today?" he asks me with one hand over his head.

"No," I say. "Just some grading and planning." I walk over to his side of the bed and sit down the bowl and the water. He grabs my hand and I sit down on the side of the bed next to him.

"Do you want me to lie here with you till you fall asleep?"

He nods and I climb over him onto the other side. I flip to my side and I spoon him from behind. I listen to the sound of the heat turn on and off and think about breakfast tomorrow and how I haven't even mentioned it to him yet.

He falls asleep quickly and the sound of his breathing, mixed with the rising and falling of his chest, leads me to gently moving off the bed away from him. I make my way to the living room and grab the stack of papers I have to grade before the weekend is over.

One in the afternoon comes and I stack everything on the kitchen table as I hear a knock on the door. I look out the eyehole in the door and see Lydia holding Abbey. I freeze, unlock the door and jerk the door open.

"Hi," she says with confusion.

"What's up?" I say, forcing a smile. Abbey throws her arms out to me and I grab her, turning back towards the kitchen.

"We were just out doing some shopping and Abbey wanted to see her Uncle Will, so I thought I'd just pop-in."

Lydia makes her way to the couch and peeks her eyes down the hallway searching for clues as to what I'm doing with my day. She turns towards me and her eyes shift from me to the kitchen table and then back to me.

"Busy day?" she asks me, folding her arms.

I make my way to the couch and set Abbey down beside me.

"Just teaching stuff," I say. "You want something to drink?"

"Sure."

I make my way back to the kitchen and I grab a bottle of water for Lydia and fill a small glass with apple juice for Abbey.

"Thank you," Abbey says, smiling up at me as I hand her the glass. I sit down on the loveseat next to the couch and arch my neck back, rubbing it.

I hear the bed creak in the bedroom and my eyes shift to Lydia who instantly spawns a smile across her face.

"Just teaching stuff, huh?"

"Shut up," I say.

"Pretty late sleeper isn't he?"

"He had a rough night."

"Oh yeah," she says, "went out with the friends. What did he say about tomorrow?"

"I haven't asked him yet," I say. She rolls her eyes and sets her water down on the coffee table. "I just forgot, honestly."

"Well, I'll just invite him myself," she says, smiling.

"I doubt he wakes up while—"

"Hey," I hear Elliot yawn out behind me. I look back and Elliot is dressed in a plain white shirt and basketball shorts. He makes eye contact with Lydia and a smile flashes across his face.

"Hey yourself," Lydia says.

"You must be the infamous sister I keep hearing about." Elliot walks closer and sits down beside me on the loveseat. "And you must be Abbey," he says. Abbey's smile glistens when she looks up at Elliot and she lets out a small giggle.

"Hi," she says, leaning into Lydia. Abbey looks up to Lydia and says, "Who's that, mommy?"

"That's your future uncle-in-law, Abbs," she says.

"Really?" I say, rolling my eyes at Lydia.

Her and Elliot erupt into laughter and Elliot grabs hold of my hand.

"Do you feel better?" I ask him.

"Yeah," he says. "Thank you."

"So, Elliot," Lydia says, uncrossing her arms and wrapping her left one around Abbey, "William and I have breakfast every Sunday morning as part of some random family tradition we started when I had Abbey. I had told him days ago to invite you, but he forgot. That or he is embarrassed of me."

"What the heck, William?" Elliot says, darting his eyes towards me and grinning.

"I really did forget," I say.

"I'd love to join you guys tomorrow," he says, looking back to Lydia.

"Awesome," she says, beaming. "I'm sorry, I didn't mean to intrude on your guys' day. We were just out and Abbey wanted to see Will, so I stopped by real quick." Lydia gets off the couch and makes her way to the kitchen. Abbey follows and I get off the loveseat and follow them to the door.

"I'll pick you up tomorrow around nine," I say, opening the door.

"Bye, girls," Elliot says from behind us.

"Say bye, Abbs," Lydia says, lifting her in her arms and looking back towards Elliot.

"Bye," she says with a little wave. She smiles and looks at me, pinching her lips together. I kiss her on the cheek and she giggles.

"Bye, guys," Lydia says and I shut the door behind them.

"I'm sorry I slept so late," Elliot says as I make my way back towards the living room.

"It's OK," I say. He moves to the couch and I sit down beside him. I wrap my arm around him and he snuggles into my chest. "Are you hungry?"

"Not really," he says, "but I should probably eat anyway."

"How about spaghetti or something? Or I have a frozen lasagna in the freezer that I've had no reason to cook for myself."

"Lasagna sounds good," he says. I get off of the couch and he groans, sliding off my shoulder onto the couch. I grab the lasagna out of the freezer and preheat the oven.

"So," I say, taking it out of the box, "I hope breakfast tomorrow is OK. She put you on the spot."

"Yeah," he says, turning his body towards me, "it will be nice."

"You really don't have to if you don't want to."

"Do you have chips or something?" he asks, getting up off the couch. He makes his way into the kitchen and opens one of the cabinet doors. "That's going to take a few hours and I actually am sort of hungry."

"You may eat whatever you please, Mr. Edwards."

Elliot comes up behind me and wraps his hands around my waist. He kisses the side of my neck and a surge runs through my body. I turn around to face him and bring my hands around his hips, bringing him closer into me.

"Hi," I say, taking his chin in my hand. I lean down and take his bottom lip in my mouth.

"I know what we can do until that's done," he says, pulling away from me. He makes his way out of the kitchen and down the hallway. I set the timer on the oven and throw the lasagna on the rack and make my way to the bedroom.

The blinds are open just enough to show the bed and Elliot standing to the right of it. He takes off his shirt and moves closer to me. He grabs my hand and sits down on the edge of the bed. I can see the outline of his cock in his shorts - hard and thick.

I take off my shirt and Elliot runs his hand down my stomach. He puts his hands around my waist and unties the loop on my pajama pants. He slides them down and my cock springs up and down into his palms. He scoots closer to me off the bed and takes me in his mouth. The pleasure surges through me and I move one hand to his shoulder and the other into his hair. I let out a moan as he takes me out of his mouth and jerks me back and forth.

He slides off his shorts and scoots me back onto the bed a few inches. I meet his eyes and he shows a hint of a smile. I move myself on top of him and devour his bottom lip again. I make my way from his mouth to his neck and he lets out a soft moan. He slowly edges back to the head of the bed and I follow his every move. I position myself in between his legs and he wraps me tighter into him. I kiss my way from his neck, down to his stomach, and kiss his hips. He moans and grabs the bed sheets on both sides of him.

He flips over and arches his back - his ass at a perfect angle for me to do with as I please. I kiss the small of his back and make my way to his middle. My cock is harder and thicker than I think it has ever been and there is pre-come oozing out of it slowly.

I gently massage his middle with my thumb and move by tongue around in circles. He moans and I strengthen the force of my thumb pushing into him. I grab a cheek in each hand and force my tongue into his middle. I move to my dresser and get the lube out of the top drawer. I squeeze some out into my palm and motion it into his middle and lather some over my cock.

I tease him, dragging my cock along the top and bottom of his ass. He tightens, and I gently shove myself into him, motioning back and forth. He moans and I shove myself deeper until my full length is inside of him.

I lean over his back and suck the bottom of his earlobe while I have my right hand in his hair, arching his neck back. He arches his back and grabs onto the back of my neck as I move in and out of him.

"Jesus," I say, letting out a hard breath, "it feels so good."

I pull out of him and he turns around, saddling my lap. He easily takes me again and wraps his hands around my head, his fingers gripping my hair, as he motions up and down on top of me. His fingers move from my head to my back and he digs into my skin. The pleasure mixed with the slight pain is amazing and I feel myself growing closer to coming.

His skin is moist from sweat and the clean scent of him fuels me even more. I lay him back and pull out of him, grabbing his cock and getting level with his stomach. I take him in my mouth and let my tongue wrap around him as I move up and down.

"I'm close," he says, arching his stomach up and resting on his elbows.

He thrusts his hips up and down, slowly, and leans his head back. He opens his mouth and lets out a soft moan as he comes into my mouth. I don't let up and his moans get louder as his back lies flat and his hips tighten. I sit up and he grabs hold of my cock. He jerks it back and forth and I let out multiple breaths as I come all over his stomach. I fall on my back beside him and close my eyes - lost in this moment with Elliot and lost in the satisfaction I feel about the fact that I'm falling in love again.

# Chapter Eleven

Elliot

"SO DID YOU GUYS DO anything exciting the rest of the day?" Lydia asks. The waitress sets down my plate of French toast and sausage and refills my glass of water.

I cut off a piece of sausage and say, "Lasagna."

"Well," Will says, "most of a lasagna. We burnt a lot of it."

"How?"

"We fell asleep and didn't set a timer," I say, thinking about waking up to the smell of smoke and dried semen all over my stomach the night before. Abbey scrapes her plate with her fork and my eyes dart up. She has jelly on the side of her face and her eyes are focused in on the piece of scrambled egg she has in her hand. I smile and look back to my food.

"So, you're an editor, Elliot?"

I look up to Lydia and nod.

"For a publishing house in the city," I say.

"I don't know how you and Will enjoy English so much," she says. "I hated it all through college. I haven't picked up a book since elementary school."

I laugh and say, "It's not for everyone. I don't know how you do what you do either. The hospital freaks me out anyway, but having to deal with people all day and patients? No thanks."

"It's more of a patience thing if anything. Which I've learned very well how to be with this one here." She picks up a napkin and wipes the jelly from Abbey's mouth. "I don't think I could do it fulltime. It gets me out of the house for a few days a week and that's good enough for me."

"I don't know why you work at all," Will says to my right. "It's not like Greg doesn't make enough money."

"It's not about the money, William. It's about having a life outside of being a mom and a housewife." Lydia gives Will a smile and says, "You'll understand one day."

She looks over at me and says, "Do you want any kids, Elliot?"

"Yeah," I say, "one day. I'd like to get myself together as far as work and all that first. Live out all my kid-less goals first."

"That's good," she says. "I was ready for Abbey. I reached that point and realized I needed something else to have a sense of purpose besides working fulltime. It was the best thing that happened to me."

"Do you ever think about having another one?" I ask her.

"Well," she says, putting a hand over her stomach, "actually—"

"***What?***" Will says, his elbows propped on the table.

"We just found out yesterday. That's why we came over."

"That's awesome!" Will yells.

Lydia looks over at me and laughs and says, "You don't have to yell, but yes, we're hoping it's a boy."

"And you're going to name it Will, right?" Will says.

"I doubt it," she says, eating her food.

Will raises his eyebrows and looks at her.

"Maybe a middle name," she says, rolling her eyes.

"You should've told us yesterday when you stopped by," he says.

"I didn't know Elliot was there or I wouldn't have showed up unannounced anyway, so I didn't want to take up anymore of your guys' time."

"It would've been a fun surprise," I say.

"Next time," she says, pointing her fork at me and laughing. "Don't forget about next weekend, Will."

He looks at her with confusion for a second and then raises his eyebrows.

"You forgot," she says.

"No," he says. "I mean, yeah, but it's still fine."

"We are going out of town for the weekend and Will is watching Abbey on Friday night."

"Oh fun," I say, smiling at Abbey.

"Do you want to help me babysit?" he says.

"Can we get pizza?" I ask him.

"Pizza," Abbey says across the table, grinning from ear to ear.

***

"I can't have kids until I figure my life out career-wise, too," Will says.

After breakfast, we make our way to the bench where we first met. The wind is heavy and the chill of the air sends goose bumps up and down my arms every time it blows towards me.

"Who said you have to have them right now?"

"I'm just sayin'," he says. "I want kids eventually, but yeah."

"How many do you want?"

"Two," he says. "A boy and a girl."

"Same," I say, smiling up at him.

The light reflects off his blue eyes and strengthens the color. His black hair shines as he runs his hands through it and leans his arm on the side of the bench. I realize that the first time I saw him sitting there weeks ago I didn't get to see the full picture.

"You're beautiful, you know that?" I say, looking over at him.

He laughs and says, "What?"

"Weeks ago when we met here, I thought you were cute, but I didn't realize how beautiful you were; your eyes and your hair. Little things, even, like the arch in your eyebrows and the way your facial hair perfectly forms on your face."

"I was really down that night," he says. "To be honest, I'm surprised I even really stopped and sat down once I saw that you were there. I don't know why I did."

"Fate."

"Maybe so," he says. I move closer to him on the bench and rest my head on his shoulder and my hand on his thigh.

"Whatever the reason," he says, "I'm thankful I did."

"Give it a few months," I say. "That's when the real me comes out: huge asshole, drains your bank account, cuts your hair while you are sleeping."

"How exciting," he says, bringing his face down and kissing me. "Thanks for coming to breakfast with me."

"Thanks for wanting me to."

He locks his fingers with mine and puts his jaw on the top of my head.

"So babysitting, huh?"

"Yeah," he says. "If you aren't comfortable doing it—"

"It will be fun," I say. "Plus, I have to get Abbey pizza now."

"We can take her to the movies or something. She is surprisingly good in public. Well, she is good in general for me, but a hellion for her mom sometimes. I think she does it on purpose - secretly a genius."

"It's exciting that they're having another one."

"Yeah," he says. He doesn't say anything else and lets out a sigh.

I lean off him and look at him.

"What?" I say.

"Her husband, Greg," he says. "He works a lot and is barely involved as it is now. Their weekend away is just a work thing that she is going with him to. I mean, he treats them well and is a fine human being and all that, but he could work less. He just chooses not to."

"How long have they been together?"

"Like ten years," he says. "Lydia used to be the same way - work was everything. One day she realized there was something else out there to do in life and he never got into the same mindset."

"I mean, if they're happy—"

"They are," he says. "I don't know. Maybe I'm just jealous."

"Of what," I say, laughing.

"I don't know. That he enjoys going to work so much and I don't. That and he's just kind of blah; truly a bore at gatherings."

"Well," I say, "good thing you have an exciting person to show off to others now."

"Cute," he says, smiling. "So, what are we going to do today?"

"Let's start with going back to your place and taking a nap."

"Just a nap?"

I get off the bench and walk around to the back. I run my fingers through his hair and look up to the sky.

"Get up and you'll find out."

***

I leave work Friday and I'm fuming. Andrew almost sabotaged the deal in London by running his mouth to the main contact that actually lives in London.

I grab my phone out of my coat pocket and call Will.

"Hello," Will says. The sound of his voice calms me a little and I let out a sigh.

"Hi," I say.

"What's wrong?"

"Nothing," I say. "Just a long fucking day. What time are they dropping Abbey off?"

"Like a half hour."

"Okay."

The silence lingers and he says, "Are you sure you're OK?"

"I'll tell you once I get there. Give me an hour or so."

"Okay, see ya in a bit."

I can't tell if I'm angrier about the fact that he almost ruined it or the fact that he has the power to ruin it. I make my way back to the apartment and Sam is eating a bowl of cereal on the couch.

"Hey," I say as I make my way down the hall into my room.

"You don't look happy," he says, making his way down the hall too. He leans one shoulder against the doorframe and lifts his bowl to his mouth with the other arm.

"Andrew," I say, grabbing my weekend bag from my closet. "He almost ruined the London thing and I'm just over it. Seeing his face every goddamn day is getting old and I'm close to being done."

"Well perk up. You got babysitting duty tonight."

"I know," I say. "Sorry, I just hate him."

"Me too, buddy," he says. "Me too.

***

The way Will is with Abbey brings a smile to my face. He's so relaxed and comfortable with her and the patience he has makes me wonder what he would be like as a father.

My mind wanders to the image of us by the beach; building sandcastles with our two kids. The sandcastle is too close to the water and the tide rolls in and destroys it. Our daughter looks at me and throws her head back and sighs. I laugh and tell her it's OK and we scoot back farther to where the tide won't get it again. Will helps our son pack the sand into his bucket and he flips it over and draws random things into it with his shovel.

"Elliot?" Will's voice draws me out of my daze and I raise my eyebrows at him in confusion.

"What?"

"Are you OK?"

"Sorry," I say, getting off the couch and grabbing my phone off the table, "I was thinking about random stuff."

I make my way back to the couch and say, "Who's ready for pizza?"

Abbey immediately turns around and gets on her feet. Her eyes grow big and she laughs. Will laughs and grabs a pamphlet off the fridge with the number of the local pizza place down the street.

I order the food and make my way to the kitchen. I take three plates and three cups out of the cabinet and set them around the table.

"Thank you," Will says behind me as he grabs some napkins off the top of the refrigerator. He grabs three forks and sets them on the table.

I lock eyes with him as he lays the forks and napkins down and say, "For what?"

"Being here tonight. Being nice to Abbey." He gives me a kiss and smiles. "Overall, just being alive in general." He looks over my shoulder to Abbey and then make to me. "Are you sure you're OK? You seem tense."

"Just work stuff," I say, shrugging my shoulders. "Specifically, my dickhead of a boss."

"What happened?"

"He just almost ruined the whole London thing by being himself. He smoothed it over after I guess, but still. I swear he is only working there out of spite against me and the rest of the staff. No one likes him; no one thinks he is qualified for his job; no one wants him there."

"Have you talked to HR about him?"

"His dad still owns a share of the company."

"Oh," he says.

"I don't know," I say, "maybe I should go somewhere else. I'm just comfortable there in despite him."

"Yeah, but you can't keep going to work and have it ruin your mood."

"I know," I say.

I make my way back to the couch and change the channel to a random animated movie. It must be one that Abbey has seen before because her eyes light up and she sits down on the couch and everything around her becomes non-existent besides the TV.

Will sits down on the other side of Abbey and lays his arm against the back of the couch. His fingers meet mine and I look over at him and smile. He grins and Abbey cuddles into his side.

***

"Is it good, Abbs?" Will says, wiping his fingers on his napkin. Abbey grins at Will and takes a drink of her juice.

My phone goes off across the room and I pay no attention to it. It goes off two more times within seconds and Will looks at me. I get off the kitchen chair and make my way over towards the couch where my phone is lit up. I see there are three messages from Andrew and I instantly get pissed.

***We need to talk!***

***As soon as possible.***

***Tonight.***

"I have to call Andrew real quick," I say, looking back towards Will.

"Okay."

He tries to manage a smile, but the anger radiating off my body is like steam off a hot spring and he knows this phone call probably won't end well. I force a smile back and try to reassure myself that Andrew isn't worth ruining this great night with Will and Abbey.

I make my way outside, onto his small patio, and shut the sliding glass door behind me. Will turns back towards Abbey and wipes her face with a napkin and I turn and look out at the building across the street.

The wind is cold and I squint my eyes as I feel my blood thicken and my heart rate increase. The leaves on the trees across the street are all almost gone and I think back to where I was last year at this time around Thanksgiving. It was my first one since the break up and going home without Drew was depressing. Specifically because it had been in the spring when it happened and I hadn't really told any member of my family yet.

They were pissed that I went so long without telling them and the whole event was just ruined when I went to my mom's and my dad's separately.

The thoughts worsen my mood and I try to shake it off and focus on why I came out here in the first place.

I tap Andrew's name on my phone and call his number. My mind is racing with thoughts as to what he needs to tell me. At this point, he could tell me he just found out that he is going to die soon and I would still be irate with him.

You can't be an asshole constantly and expect people to treat you well or accept you in general. Since day one I haven't liked him and annoyance has turned into hatred.

The phone clicks in and Andrew picks up.

"Elliot?"

"Yes," I say. "What is it?"

"It's the London deal."

My heart sinks and my blood pressure starts rising. I crack my neck to the side and firmly press my palm into the railing of the balcony.

"What about it?" I ask him.

He coughs and says, "They chose to back out of the partnership. They said that after thinking and surveying on the reading trends within the area, they don't think it is a smart move to associate themselves with our brand and the content we provide. They said the audience they are trying to reach is not located within the works that we publish."

I close my eyes and think about my hands around Andrew's throat: his face slowly turning blue and his eyes growing wide and terrified.

My one chance to stay with the company that I know like the back of my hand, in a different area no less, and the opportunity to get away from him and he ruined it.

"Nothing to do with your phone call with them earlier today then?"

"No," he says. "They just want to go in a different direction. I just thought you should be one of the first to know because I know how you were the one who they were looking to get over there to help with the start up and everything."

Is it karma? I barely wanted the opportunity until I realized that he may have jeopardized it and now, that it is no longer in my reach, I'm beyond pissed at the fact that I no longer have the opportunity.

Would they have stayed with us if I had committed sooner? Will they even speak to me now that they don't need what I have to offer?

My mind starts reeling and my anxiety skyrockets in a short span of a few seconds. I move away from the railing and sit down on the chair behind me. The chill of the cold bar sends a shock through my system, but I pay no attention to it. I sit there lifelessly with the phone to my ear and my mouth open and suddenly, the patio door opens again.

Will puts his hand on my shoulder and I slowly turn my gaze up at him. My eyes are wet and his grin slowly turns into a pained look of sadness that makes me look away.

"Can we talk about this more Monday?" I say.

"Yeah, whatever. Monday."

The call ends and I instantly rest my elbows on my knees and mash my face into my hands. I run my fingers through my hair and slowly shake my head from side to side.

"He ruined it," I say. "He ruined it all and now I'm stuck with him."

"Let's go back inside," Will says.

I get up off the chair and go to make my way back inside and Will doesn't budge. I look up at him and he wraps his arms around me and rubs the back of my neck.

He kisses the top of my head and says, "It's going to be OK."

I look up at him and his smile warms me.

Without a second thought, I swallow and say, “I love you.”

His eyes grow wide and his smile grows with them. He grabs my head on both sides and takes my bottom lip in for a kiss and says, “I love you, too.”

# Chapter Twelve

Will

MARCH COMES QUICKLY and I haven't felt better. After choosing to only teach part time and focusing my other efforts on helping build *I Am Me, You Are You*, the LGBTQ youth group that I became apart of a month back, the anxiety of not knowing what I wanted to do and what my purpose was has slowly faded away with each day that passes.

It's Friday night and I make my way home to pack for my weekend with Elliot. We were supposed to have dinner with Hadley tonight, but he moved it to tomorrow because he said he really needed to talk to me about something tonight. He sounded fine on the phone, his voice happier than he has been these past few months, but I still had a sickening feeling that something might be wrong.

Ever since he lost the opportunity to go overseas, he hasn't been the same. I can tell when he talks about work that he is almost at his breaking point. He looks exhausted as the words about what happened that day come out of his mouth, but he doesn't let it affect us. Even when I bring it up, he usually changes the subject into something more comforting.

I finish packing and make my way out to the car. The forecast called for heavy snow this whole weekend and as I pull out of the driveway, little flakes start sticking to my windshield, only to melt seconds later.

The drive to Elliot's isn't far, but the snow has already started coming down harder than expected. I eventually find a parking spot as I circle around and find someone pulling out and I take a breath before stepping outside and freezing to death.

The ground crunches beneath my feet and the wind is so heavy that I can barely see what is in front of me as I make my way inside his apartment complex.

"Snowing?" Elliot says as he opens the door.

He smiles and looks me up and down. My clothes are practically white and the thought of heat makes me plow through him into his apartment.

I move closer to the vent on the floor and slowly start removing everything wet that's on me. The heat sends a warmth up my spine and my eyes close as I get lost in the sensation of it.

I feel Elliot place his hands on my chest and I open my eyes. He smiles and slowly moves them from side to side. They graze my nipples that are hard enough to cut glass and I feel my cock tighten beneath my pants.

"I'm making dinner," he says, moving away, and I frown.

"What are you making?"

"Chicken," he says, looking inside the oven. "Barbeque chicken, specifically."

I make my way to his kitchen and look at all the food slowly cooking on the stove. The smell excites me and my stomach growls, as I make my way behind him and wrap my arms around him. I lay my head on his shoulder and take in the smell of his cologne on his neck.

"Did you have a good day?" he asks me.

"Yep," I say. "Friday's are always good because I no longer have to do anything and I get to see you."

I make my way to the cabinet and grab plates and silverware.

"Where's Sam at tonight?"

"He has a date."

"Oh,' I say. "Well that's exciting, right? It's been awhile."

"Yeah," he says. "I don't know. He doesn't have much hope for it, but he said it was best to force himself to go out and look for something again."

"He told me about his ex," I say, "months ago when we all had dinner together."

"He was a dick to Sam. I never liked the guy. I'm surprised he told you that to be honest. He doesn't open up to a lot of people about stuff like that."

"I have those tell-me-your-secrets eyes."

Elliot laughs and takes the chicken out of the oven.

"This shit is dooone," he says as he grabs two drinks out of the refrigerator.

He makes his way over to me and kisses my forehead. He sets down the drinks and picks up one of the plates. I pick up the other one and follow him in the process of stuffing my plate in excess.

"So," I say as a piece of chicken slides down my throat, "what is it you need to tell me?"

Elliot raises his eyebrows and wipes his hands on his napkin.

"Well," he says, "for starters, I quit my job today."

"Oh," I say, surprised.

"I didn't leave on the best of terms, but I couldn't do it anymore. Andrew had a meeting today with the heads of each department and he said he was going to focus less on fiction, which is what I'm in charge of, and focus more on nonfiction and other things like cook books and self-help books."

I don't say anything and instead force more food into my mouth.

"I don't know what came over me, but I stood up, looked directly at him, and said, 'Are you fucking serious?' and his jaw dropped and he just sat there with his mouth open so I just said more things like, 'This place was built on fiction being the focused genre and you just want to scrap it?' and, 'I'm done. I can't work for a place that puts you in charge. You are the worst, most annoying piece of shit that I have ever met and I honestly hope you rot in hell for all of the time that you have made me waste on you these past few years'."

"Wow," I say with a smile. "You're a badass."

"And unemployed," he says. "At least until May."

I look up at him and he has a huge grin on his face from ear to ear.

I smile and say, "Something else to tell me?"

"I got a call this morning from the London office that was wanting to do the deal with us. They explained their reasoning for everything and basically confirmed that Andrew is a piece of garbage that they want no part of."

He stops talking and starts eating again.

Almost a minute passes and I say, "And?"

"They still want me," he says. "They want me to start it from the ground up. They think I have the potential to draw in a huge audience of new and old readers." He puts down his fork and pushes his plate to the side. "It would be from May basically until September as far as getting the process going and hopefully getting a few new authors names out there. After that they said there are a lot of options they could see us doing as far as over there and over here."

"So you already said yes then?"

"Yeah," he says and I can tell that he is waiting for my reaction about the fact that he is moving across the country.

"I think it's fantastic," I say, smiling over at him.

"Really?" he says.

"Of course. You need this. You need to feel that drive again and have that reason for waking up every morning."

"It's just really huge," he says. "I'm still not sure I even believe it. Honestly, this morning when I got the call I knew as soon as I hung up the phone that this would be the day that I told Andrew to go fuck himself. I just didn't think I would be lucky enough to have something to start the conversation, but thankfully he had the meeting."

"Do they know about any of this?"

"No," he says. "I'm not going to tell anyone there about it. I don't want him calling them and trying to badmouth me or something. Not that they would listen anyway, but still, I'd rather not have all this ruined for me."

"Well why did you cancel dinner with Hadley then? Shouldn't this be something to celebrate?"

"We can celebrate with her tomorrow," he says, getting off his chair. "Tonight, I want to celebrate with you until I'm exhausted and can't celebrate anymore." He climbs on top of me and gives me the hardest kiss he ever has. He takes my bottom lip between his teeth and I feel my cock stiffen. I feel his cock spring to life under his shorts and I smile as he kisses me more.

"Well," I say, "let's go celebrate then."

***

The ground is covered in snow and our cars are invisible as we make our way down the street to the restaurant. We are both freezing and the thought of food warming my body makes my breathing quicken and my footsteps more extensive.

Elliot telling me he is moving didn't disappoint me the way that it probably should have. Maybe my happiness for him is overshadowing the sadness I feel in the fact that my days with him are limited. He didn't ask me to go with him and I wonder if he even will.

"Watch your step," Elliot says, grabbing my shoulder and bringing me closer to him on the sidewalk.

He coughs and says, "Something on your mind?"

I look over at him and smile and say, "Nope, just hungry."

His eyes are unsure, but he turns his focus back to the sidewalk and deepens into his coat.

"I haven't told anybody else about the whole London thing," he says, stepping around a fire hydrant hidden in the snow.

"Really?" I ask him surprised.

"I know they'll be happy for me, but at the same time, I don't want to see the disappointment on their faces. It's hard enough seeing it on yours."

I stop in my tracks and he throws his head back with a surprised look on his face.

"I haven't done anything to let on that I was mad about the fact that you are leaving."

"I know that's what you were thinking about back there," he says.

"Yeah," I say, slowly stepping towards him, "but I'm happy for you. I'd much rather you be hours away and happy then right beside me and unhappy."

"I'm not unhappy when I'm around you."

"I know that. That's not what I meant."

We get closer to the restaurant and there are still no cars in site. My hands have frozen in my pockets from the lack of gloves and my teeth are chattering.

"Is she even going to be able to make it?" I ask.

"Yeah," he says, taking his phone out.

He scrolls down his screen and looks at a new message from Hadley.

"She said she's walking too, so she has a few more blocks than we do."

"What do you think she'll say about it?"

"Whatever I think is best is what I should do."

"Good advice," I say, smiling.

I watch the smoke cloud of my breath wash back across my face as I lean my head back and exhale. There's a hint of tension between us now that wasn't there an hour ago, and all

I can think about now is what's going to happen once May gets here.

***

"I absolutely *hate* this fucking weather," Hadley says as she sits down across the table from Elliot and I. "I've never liked snow and I never will."

"This is a bad year for it," Elliot says as he sets down his menu and takes a drink.

"How is William today?" Hadley asks, picking her menu up.

"Absolutely *hating* this fucking weather as well."

She smiles over her menu and Elliot lets out a small cough.

"So, there's something specific that I wanted to tell you tonight," he says.

She looks from Elliot to me and back to Elliot. She sets her menu down and her eyes focus on him.

"What's wrong?"

"Nothing," he says quickly, "it's really good, actually. I quit my job."

"That's good because…"

"I got a completely new job offer in London."

Hadley's eyes widen and she opens her mouth as if to say something, but doesn't. After a few seconds she says, "That's awesome, Elliot." She looks over at me real quick and my eyes dart down to my menu immediately.

"I leave in May."

"For how long?"

"At least the summer," he says. "Just depends on how things progress."

"I've always wanted to go to London," she says. "Now I have a reason to visit. British guys are sexy as hell." She takes a drink and laughs. "Big cocks, too."

"Having a dry spell, Hads?"

"No," she says. "Well, yeah. Obviously work has become me so I haven't been properly plowed in awhile. Seeing you two love birds all the time makes me think I should get something, too."

"All my straight friends are married," I say.

"Happily?" she says. I laugh and she says, "Kidding, kidding."

"Speaking of love," Elliot says, "is Ethan still looking for that special someone."

"Yes, surprisingly. He's been seeing some guy for like a month now. He didn't tell me about it; I walked in on him making out with the guy on his couch and yeah."

"What's his name?" he asks.

"Conner," she says. "I think? Conner or Colten or Conrad or something."

"I'll have to bring it up to him," he says.

"He hasn't mentioned how big his dick is to me yet, so I think this might be a special one."

"Has he always been the promiscuous type?" I ask.

"No," Hadley says. "He just hasn't had luck with dating and after his last relationship, he basically said fuck it and started having fun. At least, he thinks of it as having fun."

"Well," Elliot says, leaning back in his chair, "if Ethan can find love again, I have no doubt in my mind that you can, too. Or at least find some dick in general."

An hour passes and we finish our food. I lean back and rub my stomach with both hands under my shirt.

"I feel awful," Hadley says, closing her eyes.

"We ate too much," Elliot says.

Hadley gets out of her chair and stretches. She turns towards us and says, "I'll be right back. Probably."

"I wonder if it snowed anymore," Elliot says.

"God, I hope not. I already can't see anything out there."

"Thanks for having dinner with me tonight."

Elliot looks over to me and his eyes are moist. He closes them and a tear runs down his cheek.

"What's wrong?" I ask him as I wipe the tear away with my thumb. He closes his eyes and sniffs.

"I'm trying to be happy about leaving, but the thought of leaving you won't stop pounding it's way through my mind and it's been bugging me all day and last night and—"

"Hey," I say, bringing his head to my shoulder. I kiss the top of his head and lean my head on his hair. "Stop worrying about us. You leaving for the summer doesn't mean we can't be together or that I love you any less."

He leans his head up and looks into my eyes and I say, "I think you've had a little too much to drink."

He laughs and says, "I know, I'm sorry. This is why I don't drink my weight when I go out. You never know which version of me you're going to get."

"Tonight is special, so you drink as much as you want. I'm not carrying you out of here, though, so maybe you should stick to water from here on out."

"I think I feel worse," Hadley says. She sits back down and pulls her wallet out of her purse.

"Excuse me," a guy says as he stops beside Hadley, "but I saw you over at the bar and saw you walk back to your seat and I just had to introduce myself."

The guy looks a little over six foot and is wearing a light blue button up with dark jeans. His hair is marine-cut and his smile makes Hadley blush as she tries to find the words to say back to him.

"Well," she says, "I'm glad you did."

He reaches out his hand and says, "Mark."

"Hadley."

She looks over at us and says, "These are my friends: Will and Elliot."

We say hello and Hadley looks back up to Mark and bites her lip.

"Well, dinner was amazing, Hads," Elliot says as he puts on his coat. "I'll talk to you tomorrow."

Hadley gets up and hugs Elliot and then embraces me as well. We make our way back outside and luckily, it hasn't snowed anymore.

"Looks like she's getting that much-needed dick tonight," I say.

"She's not the only one," Elliot says as he wraps his arm around my waist and sticks his frozen hand on my stomach.

***

Elliot pulls his underwear down and throws them towards the TV. He walks over to the couch and sits down, planting his feet firmly and slowly opening and closing the gap between his legs.

I get on my knees in the space between his legs and rub my palms up and down his thighs. He bites his lower lip and leans his head back as I kiss my way from the middle of his thigh to his hip. I kiss his stomach and slowly make my way down to his cock and lick the tip. He moans and he leans his waist into me as I take his full length in my mouth.

I massage him up and down with my hand as I drown his cock with my mouth. With one hand, he grips the side of the couch. With the other hand, he grips my head and runs his fingers through my hair. His moans grow louder as I take him deeper in my mouth and squeeze harder with the motioning.

After more strokes, I notice that the moaning stops and I look up and see his head cocked to the side, his mouth open, and his cock slowly losing blood flow.

"Wow," I say out loud with a laugh.

I lean into him and gently throw him over my shoulder and make my way to the bedroom. I lay him on the bed and cover him with the blanket. I look down at the beautiful man lying next to me and realize that the first ounce of true happiness I've experienced in awhile just fell asleep while I was blowing him and when he moves, I'm going to have to go with him.

# Chapter Thirteen

Elliot

"SOUNDS LIKE YOU HAD quite the night last night," Sam says across the table from me.

"Huh?"

"Ya know," he says, "when you feel asleep while your hot boyfriend was going down on you."

"Jesus, you heard that?"

"Yeah," he says. He clinks his fork and spoon together like a child playing with its food and looks up at me. "I can't believe you fell asleep."

"I don't even remember it to be honest, but he told me this morning before he left, so I made up for it."

"Heard that, too," he says. "Will is quite the screamer."

"This is why I like going to his place."

"At least you don't live with Ethan. He would probably come in and try to join you guys."

"Well," I say leaning back and crossing my arms, "I'm sorry you heard it regardless."

"So," Sam says with his eyebrows raised.

"So what?"

"What's this lunch meeting about?"

"Can't I just want to have lunch with my best friend?"

"Yes," he says, "but you seem nervous and you asked me last minute this morning all nervous-like."

"I got a job offer," I say.

"That's good and where—"

"London."

Sam looks at me, his mouth slightly open, and I take a drink of my water.

"Well, I mean, that's wonderful, but I thought that all fell through."

"They are still interested in me, but not everything else. They want to start an all-new publishing house with no ties to where I was. They already have a bunch of local authors and just need me to come down this summer and help set everything up and get things running."

"So, it's just for the summer?"

"I don't know," I say and my eyes dart down to the table.

"What?"

"I mean, obviously, I want to go, no questions asked."

"But you are worried about Will?"

"Yeah.

"Why?" he says.

"I don't know. We are still relatively new, and of course I wouldn't expect him to go with me and even move over there, but

I also know that I can't stay here if I do have the opportunity to do something big."

"You'd just have to ask him. Assuming you would actually want him to come with you. Plus, almost six months is a little more than relatively new."

"All the guys I've dated, I've never liked, let alone loved, them the way I love Will. He's just…different. I feel comfortable and at peace and at home with him and the idea of him not being in my life terrifies me quite honestly. Everything is coming together as far as my career and all that's left is having that special someone and Will is that person."

"Then ask him. It's not like he is going to invite himself."

I look outside the window past Sam's head and see traffic backed up. People are maneuvering through the cars like a maze to rush off to wherever they need to go and I blankly wonder what all the stress of it is for. I wonder if London is just as cluttered and busy and filled with people who just do the same thing everyday in a robotic fashion with their coffees and lattes and cellphones pressed against their ears while they walk and run to wherever they think they're meant to be in that moment.

"I like Will. Elliot?" Sam snaps his fingers in front of my face and I slowly look back over to him. I laugh and close my eyes and then slowly open them.

"I wasn't paying attention."

"Clearly," he says. "I said, I like Will. I think he's great for you honestly. You say you haven't felt this strongly for a person before and that's saying something at least. If you want your career and the love of your life then all you need to do is ask him. I highly doubt the idea of going with you hasn't crossed his mind."

"He just got his new thing going here and stuff, too. I don't want to make him feel like he has to give that up just to be with me."

"Well," he says, "even if he doesn't want to go with you, that doesn't mean you have to break up. Long distance relationships exist for reasons like this one."

"So, how are things in Sam's world?"

"Good," he says and puts his hands behind his head. "I finished up some more covers with your old team, but I actually got a new job offer at a game studio yesterday where I'll handle all their media-related designing, but also get to help with the actual animation side of things."

"Now ***that*** is an exciting opportunity!"

"I mean it's not as exciting as getting to go to London," he says, laughing, "but it's in a field I love, so I'm very excited. Plus it's a full-time thing. No more freelance bullshit or vampire novels. Well, I will probably still do freelance in my free time. The money can be good and those rich housewives need someone to help design things for their shitty books."

"I'm happy for you, Samuel."

"Well, I'll be even happier for ***you*** once you tell your boyfriend you can't live without him."

I smile and wonder if Will really would go with me. There's a lot here that he wouldn't want to walk away from, but there's also a lot here that he would want to walk away from I imagine.

"Now you just need a man in your life."

"No," he says.

"But—"

"I like being career-driven only for the time being."

"Don't you miss it though?"

"What, being cheated on and giving my all only to get fucked and not in a good way?"

"Well," I say, "don't you at least miss getting fucked ***in*** the good kind of way?"

"I don't think about it much."

"You also never had a good sex-life with any of your partners."

"Exactly, so I've never expected much and don't feel the need to get any."

"But, and just hear me out, if you did find someone that was good, then maybe you would want to actually have it like normal people."

"I'll download an app or two. Happy?"

"Yes."

"So, have you told Hadley?"

"Told her last night. She was thrilled, but she also was in an overly excited mood. And she got some dick last night, too."

"And Ethan?"

"No."

"Why haven't you told him yet?"

"Because I know he won't be happy about it."

"I don't know, El. He's been acting different lately. The selfish, slutty Ethan that we all know and love is slowly going away."

"I know that version of him too and he still won't be thrilled by the fact."

Sam looks at me and rolls his eyes.

"I'll tell him tonight, we're having dinner. He met someone I guess."

"Another double date?"

"No, he's saving this one he said."

"Well, find out his name at least and ill stalk him on social media."

Sam's phone buzzes on the table and his face tenses up as he reads the message.

"I gotta go. Your old, cocksucker of a boss needs to get my signature on some things before tomorrow and needs to see me." He turns the phone around and once I look at it, he says, "ASAP!"

"Have fun," I say. "I'll get this."

"Thanks, buddy."

Sam gets up and gets a few feet to the door when he stops in his tracks. He speed walks back over to me and strains a smile and says, "Don't freak out."

"What's—" I look past Sam towards the entrance and see Drew standing just in front of it. He's frozen in place and locked in on me.

I look up to Sam and say, "Go."

"You sure?"

"I'm fine."

I get my wallet out and set my card on the receipt.

"Hi," I hear Drew say beside me as the waiter takes the bill.

I look up at him and say, "I heard you've been back for awhile."

"Yeah," he says and looks down at the floor towards his feet.

"Do you want to sit?"

He sits down and looks up at me, his eyes getting moist.

"Words can't begin to describe how sorry I am for everything. I just—"

"I don't want an apology," I say, cutting him off. He looks down at the table and takes a breath. "But I will take answers. Like what happened and why you just up and left everything like someone on the run."

"Do you remember my friend from high school that I came here with years ago? The one who was like a brother to me?"

"Yeah."

"He died a few days before I had left that year. I couldn't handle it. I had other things going on with work and we weren't doing great either and him dying just really messed me up."

"Where did you go? Just back home?"

"You'd think that would make it worse, but it didn't. Being here reminded me of him in ways that I didn't want to think about, but back there, I remembered things that shaped me and all the positive things that happened when he actually was in my life. I didn't think about anything when I left."

"I just wish you would've came to me about it; any of it. How you were feeling. I mean, I get that you were messed up, but you just up and left without any reason as to why." The tears start to run down his face and he looks up at me.

"I'm not mad anymore," I say. "I don't even know if I was mad at you at all. To be honest, we did have problems and you leaving solved a lot of them."

He laughs and I say, "Sorry, that sounded horrible."

"It's fine," he says. "I mean, you're right. You didn't deserve it, but I just wasn't all there to really tell you anything. I don't even remember driving back home. That week in general is all a blur."

He wipes his nose just as the waiter brings back my card and says, "He meant a lot to me. Not in a relationship kind of way or anything, but he was always there for me when we were young. His family became my family. I owe him a lot. He helped me accept being gay too in the way he was so comfortable with myself. We didn't talk as much once we moved here, but we'd still have dinner occasionally. Work took over and we got new friends. We drifted and I hate that."

"How'd he die?"

"A really bad car crash. Evan was driving back to the city one night I guess and someone hit him head on; a dumb fucking drunk driver that survived it all unscathed. At least, that's what his fiancé and family were told. I never met the guy, but saw pictures. They were together for a while; three or four years I think. Had planned to get married a month after the crash happened, but yeah."

My stomach drops and I know I'm just overthinking, but I look at him anyway and say, "What was his fiancés name?"

"Um, Will, I think? Forget his last name. He seemed like a nice guy. Still lives here I think. Evan's family hasn't really talked to him from what I hear."

I feel sick and am frozen in place for a few seconds. I take a deep breath and Evan looks back up to me.

"You OK?"

"I'm glad you're safe. And back, thanks."

"For what?"

"For telling me everything. I have to go, but I'll see you around probably. The city is only so big."

"Bye, El."

I make my way outside and my vision goes a little blurry. I make my way around the corner and lean against the wall. I don't know why I'm so anxious about what he said. I knew they were close, Will told me everything; except for the fact that they were engaged ***and*** getting married ridiculously close to when Evan died.

I make my way towards the apartment, trying to process my thoughts and not freak out over nothing. Just as I get to my building, I stop and look at the sidewalk. I feel the bile come up and vomit goes everywhere. I wipe my mouth and make my way into the apartment and get a glass of water.

My phone dings and I see it's a message from Ethan.

***What time do you want to meet for dinner?***

***6 or 7.***

***OK. I'll pick you up between 6 and 7, friend.***

I set the phone back down and make my way to my bedroom. I lay my cheek against the pillow and look out the window. It's not like Will lied to me, he just didn't tell me everything. But why didn't he tell me everything? One of the most important things about his relationship with Evan and he just didn't include it.

My heartbeat slows down and my stomach becomes less of a mess and the light slowly fades from my view as I fall asleep.

***

I wake up from my nap and see it's almost six-thirty. I go into the kitchen and look at my phone and see a missed call from Will and a message from Ethan that he is going to be late. I get another glass of water, grab my phone and make my way to the couch.

I call Will and each ring makes me more and more nervous. He'll be able to tell the nervousness in my voice and I don't know what I'll say to him.

"Hello," he says.

“Whatcha doin’?”

“Watching TV. What are you doing, lover?”

“Just got up from a nap. Waiting for Ethan to get here. Going out to dinner.”

“Think he’ll be happy about everything?”

“Underneath it all,” I say, laughing, “but he’ll be unhappy I’m sure. He met someone apparently.”

“Well that’s good.”

“Hopefully.”

“You OK?” he says. My stomach turns and I yawn.

“Yeah,” I say. “Still just really tired. I need to get ready honestly, so I’ll call you later.”

“Okay,” he says. “Love you.”

“Love you, too.”

A half hour later, I hear a bang on my door and Ethan walks in.

“Ready, fucker?”

***

“His name is Cody,” he says. “He’s pretty ***and***, you’ll be happy to know, he isn’t a complete idiot.”

I smile and say, “Both is good.”

“He’s a nurse. I met him when I was doing some work for the hospital.”

“Someone to take care of you.”

He laughs and says, “Hopefully in other ways and not in a doing-his-job kind of way.”

“I have to tell you something,” I say, putting my arms across my chest.

He picks up his menu and says, "Yes, Elliot?"

"I got a job offer in London."

"Yeah, the one that fell through."

"No," I say.

He looks up and raises his eyebrows.

"Same people," I say, "but they just want me now. Nothing to do with where I was at or the dickhead who ran the place."

"Oh," he says and looks back down at the menu. "Well, that's wonderful, Elliot."

"Huh?"

"What?"

"I was expecting you to act a little differently."

"I mean, I'm not thrilled about the fact that you are leaving, but it's what's best and I'm sure the opportunity is once in a life time."

"It is."

"And Will?"

"What about him?"

"How did he react?"

"Same as you, honestly," I say. "Thinks it is great and didn't say anything about me leaving, but I'm assuming he isn't thrilled either."

"Have you asked him about going with you?"

"No," I say.

"Um, why?"

"I don't know how to ask him. That's a big thing. He'd be uprooting his life."

"Maybe he cares enough about you to go with you. Ask yourself, would you go with him if the situation was switched?"

I hadn't thought of that before now. Would I?

"Yes," I say, without a doubt. "I don't expect him too, though."

"But he might even want to go with you; to experience all these new things with you. To start his life with you in general even if it's not here."

"Damn," I say.

"What?"

"Cody has had quite the affect on you."

He rolls his eyes and leans his elbows on the table. "No," he says. "Honestly, I've just been thinking about things differently and trying to think more like an adult rather than a child like I have been."

"I wouldn't say child."

"I haven't been acting the way I should as far as interacting with certain people. Haven't been treating myself right."

"So, tell me more about him."

"Well we met at the hospital and I didn't even know he was gay until we got to talking and I said something about girls and he corrected me and laughed and then we made plans for dinner and yeah."

"What's his last name?"

"Why?"

"I don't know," I say, laughing.

He pulls out his phone and brings up his profile on Facebook. He hands me the phone and says, "Creep away."

"Jesus, he's gorgeous."

"I know. The fact that he is smart and has a real job makes it even better. But that's not why I like him, honestly. He's nice and comfortable."

"He makes you feel good for reasons that you can't explain or haven't experienced before?"

"Yeah," he says, laughing.

"That's how Will is for me."

"I've had a bad run of guys and this one just feels different. The past few months with him have been nice."

"Wait," I say with a laugh, "you've known this fucking guy for months and are just ***now*** bringing up the fact that he exists."

"I wanted to make sure it was something real. Not another Paul or another late-night-pound in general like the others."

"Well I'm glad it's working out. Maybe you found something good for once."

"We haven't had sex yet either."

"Shut up," I say.

"Seriously," he says. "We've kissed, but nothing else."

"That must be hard for you."

"It's always hard, El."

"So, what's the problem?"

"I just want to take it slow. New me, new choices."

"But months?"

"I plan to do something soon. He hasn't pushed. We've talked about it and he gets it."

"Have you talked about certain ***things*** like your history and such?"

"He knows about Rick a little. He know some of the things that happened, but not the super messed up parts."

"Well that's good. You don't tell a lot of people about that."

"I know. But yeah, he's pretty great so far, so we will see I guess."

The night goes on and he eventually asks, "So, when do you start this job of yours?"

"Late May, early June."

"Wow," he says, "that's soon."

"Yeah."

"Is it just the summer like before?"

"They want me down there to start it up, but I have no doubt they'll want me there long-term."

"And you'll end up staying?"

"Probably," I say.

"Then you need to tell Will that. I have no doubt that he'll go."

"He has his sister here, though, and his niece and he just started his new job."

"They'll survive and I'm sure there are countless people over there that he can help out."

"Jesus, I completely forgot about earlier and haven't told you. I saw Drew."

"Shuuuut the fuck up," he says. "Where?"

"Me and Sam had lunch earlier and he just walked on in."

"What'd he have to say?"

"He told me why he left which makes things even more interesting."

"And?"

"Basically this guy he used to be really close with died and it messed him up and he couldn't handle life anymore so he moved back home."

"Why is that interesting?"

"The friend who died was Will's ex who died in that car crash."

"Whatever."

"I swear to God."

"What'd Will say?"

I look down across the room to every random set of eyes I can find and zone back in on Ethan.

"You haven't told him," he says.

"No."

"Why?"

"Because they were engaged and he never told me that."

"That's odd."

"Right? I mean, what the fuck? Why didn't he tell me that?"

"I'm sure there's a valid reason. Will isn't a bad dude."

"I don't even know how to bring it up. It's awkward really. I just don't know why he didn't mention the fact. I mean, it's kind of a big deal, right?"

"Just talk to him about it I guess. Maybe it reminds him too much of it all and it makes it too real or some deep shit like that."

"I don't know," I say, rubbing my eyes. "I'm glad we had dinner tonight. I don't get to see you guys as much now I feel like."

"Well if you weren't stuck up your boyfriend's ass all the time."

"I know," I say.

"I don't blame you," he says. "I'd probably want to be all over that ass, too. That nice, delicious, firm—"

"I get it," I say, cutting him off, "you think he's hot. Can you believe I fell asleep last night while he was trying to blow me?"

"That good?"

"Too much alcohol," I say. "We met Hadley last night and I drank too much."

"So I'm the last one you told then," he says.

"The best for last."

"Awe," he says. "You're so full of shit."

"She actually left with a guy."

"I heard all about him this morning when she stopped by. She said she finally got some much-needed dick and I could tell. She seemed happy as fuck. Made me want to invite Cody over and get some as well."

"How much longer are you going to wait?"

"Not much longer," he says. "A few days probably. A few hours, he's coming over once I leave here."

I smile and say, "We better get you home then."

"Right," he says. "Seriously though, El, talk to Will."

# Chapter Fourteen

Will

I WAKE UP IN A SWEAT. The dreams about Evan went away months after the accident, but I still sometimes get them here and there and they leave me anxious and exhausted in the morning when they finally end.

I look over to my phone and see it's almost eight in the morning. I go into the bathroom and splash some water on my face to wake myself up and look in the mirror. I haven't shaved in days and any other time I would have said enough is enough, but Elliot likes the beard and I like Elliot.

I put on a pair of shorts and a cut-off shirt, grab my ear buds and make my way outside. I stretch out my legs on the sidewalk and think about what Elliot is doing at this time in the morning. Most likely sleeping I imagine, and I smile.

I make my way down my street and onto Elliot's. As I go past his apartment, I see Sam leaning into his car.

"Searching for something?" I say as I take the ear buds out.

"Hey, man," he says, smiling up at me as he turns his head. "I lost this person's fucking business card and I can't find it and I have no other way to contact him and I'm ready to blow my brains out. What are you up to?"

"Just running," I say.

"You should get your boyfriend to do that sometime. Lazy-ass sleeps forever and then reads or eats or watches TV."

"I love a man that wastes the day away," I say, tilting my head back.

"Is he OK? I figure yesterday was a bit much for him and I haven't heard from him since."

"I didn't know anything was wrong," I say, confused.

What happened to Elliot that he didn't tell me yesterday?

"Oh," he says.

"I mean, is it something serious? Did he get hurt or something?"

"No," he says. "Honestly, you should talk to him about it. He'd probably be pissed if I said anything. It's really fine. Just...talk to him."

I make my way into the apartment and see Elliot on the couch eating a bowl of cereal as I open the door.

"Find it?" he says.

"Still looking," I say and he quickly turns his head my way.

"Hey, babe," he says with a mouth of Cheerios. I make my way to the couch and sit down beside him and he attempts a smile through the food.

"What are you doing here?" he says.

"Was out for a run and ran into Sam. He asked me if you were OK."

His face turns back towards the TV and he shakes his head from side to side quickly.

"I'm fine," he says. He focuses on the TV and doesn't look in my direction again.

"Well, something happened yesterday if you might not have been OK."

"I saw my ex."

I skip a breath, look from him to the TV and say, "Oh."

"It was unexpected and I was, and I am, fine. Just wasn't planning to see him and it was a bit much. Sam saw him first before he left the restaurant. Only reason he knows."

"Did he say anything about leaving?"

"Are you hungry?" he says, trying to change the subject.

"If you don't want to talk about it that's—"

"I just don't want to right now. We can talk later at dinner about it. Okay?"

"Okay. And I could eat, but I'll wait till I'm done."

I get up off the couch and make my way to the door.

"You don't have to go."

"No, I need to get this out of the way and then I have a bunch of stuff to do before dinner for tomorrow. I plan to do other things after dinner rather than work stuff."

He winks at me, smiles and says, "Bye, William."

I make my way back outside and see that Sam is gone. I look towards the opposite way of my apartment, but turn around and go back home because the knot in my stomach and the curiosity about Elliot's ex has ruined the idea of exercising for me.

I get back to the apartment and once I'm in the doorway, I just stand there frozen. I don't feel nervous, but the thoughts about what happened are nonstop and I try to focus in on the now and bring myself back so I don't get a headache.

It's fine, he's fine. If it had been serious, he would've called me yesterday once it happened.

I hop in the shower and sit on the floor on the tub. I wrap my arms around my knees and lay my head on top of them.

Wondering what Drew said to Elliot eats at me as each passing second goes by and each drop of water touches my skin. The water is hot, but it doesn't warm my skin. I feel cold and confused and the worry starts to get to me for no reason.

I don't know if the thoughts come because I think he may go back to him or if I'm anxious about the fact because of how he left and all I can do is wonder why.

I focus to the night I met Elliot on our bench and smile. He didn't know it, but I stood there for a couple minutes before I decided to sit down. I looked from the city and the bridge to him and saw the lights reflect off his face and the way his features curved into the beautiful shape of his face. He ran his hand through his hair and let out a breath and I decided to sit down instead of deciding to keep on walking. I wouldn't normally have sat there in the middle of the night if someone was there, but I didn't feel uneasy or odd about the fact.

I knew once I saw him that I had to try to find someone again. To cure the ache that Evan's passing had left on me. To actually try and accept the fact that Evan was in fact gone and it was time for me to move on as well.

I get off the floor and actually do what I got in the shower to do. It's still early, so once I get out, I make my way to the bed and sit on the edge of it. I check my phone for messages while I was in the shower and see there is one from Elliot.

***You really didn't have to leave.***

I put the phone back down and put some clothes on.

***I know. I really do have a lot to do before tonight.***

I go to the living room where there are piles of random paperwork scattered around the room. Most of them just need my signature, but I also have to review multiple people that we interviewed earlier in the week for counseling positions. It all will only take me a few hours, but Elliot doesn't have to know that.

***OK. Pick me up around 6?***

***Yes, sir. Love you.***

***Love you too.***

I turn my phone on vibrate and flip it over so I can focus on the work I have to do. This new job has kept me busy, but in a good way. Teaching left me with things towards the end that I had no motivation to do, but things for this always have a purpose and in a lot of ways affects and helps the teenagers that come to us.

All of the people we interviewed had plenty of experience, but only a few showed interest in helping the kids I felt. At the end of the day, I'd rather have someone with less experience if they had the urge to help more than just be there for someone to talk. I already knew who I thought was the best fit once the interviews were over.

I still look over all the candidates again, but I still pick Deb. Deb is in her mid-thirties and has a daughter going through the process of discovering herself. She'd been tormented at school and when they wouldn't help, Deb took it upon herself to move her to a different school and look into organizations like ours for help. She also has worked in multiple schools as a counselor and her references were nothing short of amazing.

I put her information to the side and stack the rest of them in a pile. I move onto everything that needs signed which takes me no time at all. I look back at my phone and see that only an hour and a half has passed and I lay back against the couch and roll my eyes.

I won't bring anything up to Elliot; I'll let him bring it all up so it's not awkward. My nervousness doesn't come back about the subject, but I still can't wrap my brain around what exactly they would've talked about and I really can't decide why it bothers me so much thinking about the fact.

***

I make my way to Elliot's and try not to think about all the stupid thoughts that have crossed my mind today. Everything is fine and will remain fine. I have to trust what Elliot says.

"Hey," Elliot says as he shuts the door to my car. It's six on the dot and he is nothing but smiles.

"You look nice," I say, leaning over and giving him a kiss.

"I took a nap earlier, so I had the motivation to at least look a little good for you."

"You're so thoughtful to think of me, Elliot."

"I'm starving. All I had was that cereal."

"Jesus," I say, "how long was your nap?"

"Well, I ate and then I watched some TV and Sam came back and I napped and then I got up and showered and went back to sleep and then got back up and yeah."

"So, two naps then?"

"Maybe," he says. He grabs my hand and holds it, setting it on his knee. "I promise you, I'm fine." I look over at him and he's looking straight ahead into the traffic.

"I know," I say and he looks over at me and smiles.

We make it to the restaurant and get sat at a table in the back. The room is dark and calming and the temperature is cool to where I'm glad I brought a jacket with me.

"I've never been here before," he says.

"Me either. Thought we'd try something new."

"New is good," he says and picks up his menu. He looks over the menu and into my eyes for a split second and I instantly get a hint of nerves, but they go away just as fast as they hit.

"He told me why he left," he says.

He sets down his menu and puts his hands together in a fist on the table. He looks up at me and raises his eyebrows.

"Was the reason satisfying enough?"

"It actually made me feel worse," he says.

"Oh," I say, looking down at his hands. The anxiety rises in my stomach again, but I focus back on him.

"He left because he had a friend that died and he couldn't handle the loss. It really messed him up. To be honest, we had problems anyway and we weren't going to last, but, obviously, him up and leaving still hurt."

I don't say anything and he continues.

"The friend died in a really bad car accident. He left days after."

"Well, I'm sure it must have been hard on him if he up and left. He probably wasn't in the right state of mind to think about anything."

He doesn't say anything and lets out a heavy breath.

"Why did it make you feel worse?"

"When I say this, don't freak out. Try to remain somewhat relaxed and just let me get it all out."

"Okay?"

"His friend's name was Evan."

My stomach instantly drops and I close my eyes.

"What does that have to do with me?" I ask him, but I already know the answer.

"I wouldn't have just assumed it was your Evan except he brought up the fact that his *fiancé* was a man named Will who he was getting ready to get married to in a few weeks, but then the accident happened."

"Elliot, I—"

"What bothered me," he says, "is the fact that you haven't mentioned once that you guys were engaged. I can't wrap my brain around the fact that you just decided not to tell me. If it's because it makes it too hard on you then that's OK. If you just didn't think about the fact then that's OK, too. But if you didn't tell me for others reasons like not trusting me or something like that, then it really bothers me. We've been together for awhile now, so I'm just confused as to why I don't know this already."

I look down at the table and focus on a small cut that goes into the wood. I think about how it got there and who or what did it and if they even realize that they damaged something that was once whole.

"Drew hadn't talked to Evan for awhile," he says, "so I wouldn't have assumed you would've met him or anything. The fact that this is all connected is crazy anyway, but all I can think about is that you were going to get married."

"I didn't tell you because it *does* make everything worse," I say.

My eyes start to water and I look towards the bar-area at people laughing and having fun. I make eye contact with Elliot and immediately look back down at the table and say, "I had to switch grocery stores a few months back. It was actually after I had met you that night and I went to the store that I've been going to since I moved here. I saw Evan's sister there, who I hadn't talked to in awhile because I shut them all out, and I left the store in the midst of a panic attack. I left a cart full of groceries by the registers and a store full of people probably wondering if they were watching someone go insane."

I look up to him and his face is relaxed. His eyes are moist and they don't leave mine. I look back down and say, "I had a really hard time when he passed. I didn't think I was going to make it. I went to a therapist and took some medicine and it helped, but the attacks didn't go away for a year and then I saw her. My heart was broken when I met you to the point where I didn't think I would ever find someone again. I still love Evan, immensely. He was the best person in the world as far as I was concerned and not having the chance to marry him and get to spend my life with him hurt just as much as anything."

The waitress comes over for our orders and Elliot orders for the both of us. She notices that I'm crying, but doesn't say anything as Elliot assures her that I'm fine with his hand and eyes.

"I didn't tell you because it hurt too bad. The more serious we got, the more I forgot about the fact and then I would've never told you anyway because I never would have thought to."

He grabs my hand and I look up at him. He smiles and says, "I'm sorry I ruined our dinner with this."

"I'm sorry I gave you a reason to wonder why I kept something from you."

"I don't know why it bothered me so much," he says. "I think it was a mixture of the shock of seeing Drew and then my brain completely fucked itself when I found out everything. I am just exhausted, really, over the last few days. I've made a big deal over nothing."

"I did the same thing earlier wondering what Drew said to you," I say. "Curiosity at it's best."

"I want you to know, I don't want you to lose the love you have for Evan. The fact that you were able to care for someone so deeply is a beautiful thing and I know you'll probably always have a part of yourself missing because he's gone. I know I can't completely fix what's broken, but I can promise you, I'll never stop trying."

"You've done a good job so far," I say. I run my fingers through my hair and laugh and say, "Well that was a nice and awkward beginning to the night. I'm surprised I didn't just freak out to be honest. Usually things like that would make me think about him and bring on the bad memories. I haven't really had anything like that happen since the beach."

"Well, that's good."

"It's because of you," I say.

"I don't thin—"

"No," I say, "it is because of you. Just…thank you, Elliot. For everything and for being in my life in general, really. You've done things for me that you'll never be able to realize and for that, I will always be grateful. Meeting you was the best thing that has ever happened to me."

"You're welcome, William."

He smiles and the grin reaches his eyes. The waitress brings our food and he thanks her as I'm lost in the features of his face. The beautiful, breathless face of Elliot Edwards.

# Chapter Fifteen

Elliot

"I LEAVE AT THE END of May," I say to Will who is sitting across the table from me.

"Do you have to go over before that for anything? To sign something or anything like that?"

"Nope," I say. "They have housing set up for me there already, too. A nice two-bedroom."

Will looks back down at his food, takes a bite and looks out the window.

"Hopefully it's a nice place," he says.

"They sent me some pictures."

"Show me," he says, smiling.

I pull out my phone and show him the email from them with all the pictures.

"I like the countertops in the kitchen; the granite blends well with everything else. All hardwood floors, though, that sucks."

"Shit's cold," I say.

"Yeah," he says.

He hands the phone back to me and goes back to his food.

It's only a few more weeks until I leave and I still haven't asked him to come with me. It's not because I don't want him to, but I don't think there is a right moment to ask him and I'm too much of a pussy to ask him in general. Things are also still weird because of the whole engagement talk we had nights ago. He says it's fine, but I know it made him uncomfortable because it made me uncomfortable and I didn't even have a reason to be.

I put my phone on the table and look over at him again. I watch the way his jawline moves as he takes each bite and the way his eyes give a hint of a squint as he focuses on something outside.

He looks over at me and makes eye contact.

He smiles and says, "Yes, Elliot?"

"Just watching you," I say.

"You didn't eat very much."

"I'm not hungry," I say.

My stomach has been in knots since I found out when I leave. Not just because of the Will situation, but moving to a different country and not knowing how long you'll be there is stressful and I feel like I'm going in to it all without any sort of clue whatsoever about what my future holds.

"What's wrong?"

"Nothing," I say.

"Elliot," he says, raising his eyebrows.

"Just a lot of stuff going on in the next month and a half. I have a lot to do before I go. I wouldn't be as stressed if I knew how long I was going to be over there for."

"I mean, you can always come back to good old America if you get sick of the place. But I see them wanting you to stay long term."

"I know," I say. "That's what I'm nervous about because I already know I don't want to stay long term. I've been thinking more about it. But that might change once I'm over there. I don't know."

This surprises Will and his eyes grow wide for a split second and then back to normal. He takes a drink of water and says, "Is this because of me?"

"No," I say, because it's true. "It's an exciting opportunity and I really want to go over and experience life there for a little bit, but they haven't mentioned at all me staying there permanently and I already know I'll tell them no if they ask which I hope won't ruin anything. My life is here. My friends are here."

He looks down at his food and back up to me.

"You're here," I say.

"Maybe they'd let you do some things from over here once you do come back. Read manuscripts and things like that. You don't have to be there really to give feedback and edit. Hell, they might even want to open an office over here and you could run it. Branch out the company and gain a wide variety of writers and readers."

"I doubt it," I say, "but maybe."

"It will all be fine. They have a lot of faith in you already. If they see half the perfection that I see in you, they'll be offering you all sorts of shit. Plus you said when they first offered you it that they had ideas for all sorts of possibilities, so don't worry about it. Okay?"

He sits his plate to the side and puts all the trash from the table on top of it. The waitress brings over the check and he takes it out of her hand before I can even see it in her hand.

"You ready?"

"Whenever you are," I say.

Will gets out his wallet and throws enough cash on the table to cover our meals plus a tip.

"You just paid for our dinner the other night, too," I say.

"I don't mind," he says.

"Makes me feel like I'm not contributing anything," I say.

"Well, how about we get back home and I'll let you contribute in anyway you like?"

***

Will walks straight back to his bedroom when we get back to his apartment and I laugh as he takes off a different piece of clothing as he makes his way through the living room and down the hallway; his pants tossed on the couch, shirt thrown on the lamp by the TV, socks by the bathroom door, underwear outside of his bedroom door.

I walk into his room and he is already under the covers with the blanket covering just below his stomach. He smiles at me and slightly jerks his head motioning me to come closer.

I take off my shirt and watch his eyes slowly move up and down my body and I reach for my zipper on my pants. My cock is hard under my boxer briefs and his eyes gaze down to the outline of it as I take off my pants. I walk over to the right side of the bed that he is on and he grabs my cock as soon as I am within reaching distance.

I bend down to kiss his lips and he bites my bottom lip as he tugs on my cock.

He pulls down my underwear and bends his head down, taking me in his mouth. The sound of his lips smacking as he motions back and forth makes the pleasure even greater and I rest my right hand on the nightstand and he doesn't let up.

Fully erect, I pull his head up to look at me and stick my tongue in his mouth. He moans and scoots over in the bed as I get underneath the covers. I grab his cock and smooth my thumb over his tip as I make my way from his mouth to his neck. He moans and puts his hand in my hair as I move from the left to the right of his neck.

He slowly flips over and curves his body – planting his ass straight up in a perfect alignment with my front. I run my hands down both cheeks and circle my right thumb in between them. I spread both cheeks wide and he sends out several loud moans as I stick my tongue in between them and prepare to untighten him.

I reach under and grab his cock, motioning it back and forth. I force his cock back and suck on the tip as I smooth my thumb in circles between his cheeks. He moans and I smile as some pre-come drips from his dick. I lick it up and make my way back to untightening him.

I rub my own cock back and forth and squirt some lube from the bottle on the nightstand into my hand. I lather my own cock in it and rub the rest around his rim. I slowly ease myself in and back out as I watch Will's head arch back and a moan escape his lips.

As he gets more comfortable, I shove my whole length into him and he says, "Oh fuck."

I smack into him, slow at first, and slowly speed up until I'm moving in and out without effort. The pleasure is amazing and I pull out of him and flip him back over. He arches his legs back and I add some more lube and push myself inside of him again. His head deepens into the pillow as he bites his bottom lip and grabs ahold of his cock with his hand.

He uses his other hand to rub my chest and my motions speed up as I watch him relish in pleasure. His eyes move down to his cock and he says, "I'm gonna come."

I pound into him harder and faster and he moans and says, "So good."

He shoots onto his stomach and deepens his head into the pillow again as he massages his tip and his moans echo through the room. I go to pull out and he locks his legs around my waist.

"No," he says, "come in me. Enjoy it."

I let out a deep moan as I unload inside of him and he motions back and forth. The pleasure is unrelenting and I fall on top of his stomach and close my eyes.

"That was fantastic," he says. "Jesus, that was good."

I pull out of him and smile as I look down at him and plant a kiss on his lips.

I make my way to the bathroom and turn on the shower. I hear the bed creek and the next thing I know, his hands are wrapped around me and his head is rested against my neck.

"I love you," I say, leaning my head back and kissing him.

"Same," he says, getting into the shower. I get in behind him and stand there with my arms wrapped around his waist and my head against his back. I think about the fact that the idea of not having this man in my life feels like torture and letting the thought of time away from him in another country make me so anxious and worried about our future is stupid.

He turns around and rests his chin on the top of my head and we stand there for what seems like forever.

***

I wake up and see we slept for a couple hours after we got out of the shower. Will is still asleep so I slowly make my way out of the bed and into the kitchen for some water. I hear Will's phone ring as I make my way back down the hallway towards his room.

"What?" I hear him say as I get a few feet from the door. "Are they OK? Which hospital? Which room?"

I walk into his room and see him putting on his pants and shirt.

"Okay. Yes, i'm leaving here right now." He looks up to me and his eyes are filled with tears.

"What is it?"

"That was Greg," he says. "Lydia and Abbey were in an accident. He says they're OK, but Lydia got pretty banged up."

"I'll drive you," I say, moving towards my phone on the opposite side of the bed.

"No," he says. "I mean, I can drive there, it's fine. I'll be fine, I just need to get there."

"Are you su—"

"Yes," he says, making his way out of the bedroom. Seconds later, I hear the front door slam shut and I sit on the edge of the bed wondering what I should do.

I make my way to the living room and sit on the couch. I dial Ethan's number and wait for him to pick up as I try to focus on the situation.

"Hello?"

"Hey," I say.

"What's up?"

"Something happened. Will's sister and niece were in a wreck. I was going to drive him there, but he said no and just left and I don't know whether to stay here and wait for him or leave or go there anyway or what."

"Are you OK? You sound upset."

"I'm just confused. He really didn't want me to go with him."

"Did you drive there?" he asks.

"No," I say, remembering I walked.

"I actually just left from your place, I was seeing Sam. I can come pick you up and we can talk about it or I can take you to the hospital or something."

"Ok," I say.

"Be there in a minute," he says.

***

"I'm sure he didn't mean anything by it," Ethan says as we make our way into the city.

"I know," I say. "He was just so quick to say no and it just surprised me, that's all. He was really upset and I get that. Just didn't figure he'd push past me like that without saying anything else."

We eventually make our way down towards the pier. Ethan parks his car and we walk the rest of the way to an overlook over the water.

"Has he text you or anything? Surely he made it by now."

"No," I say, checking my phone again. I make sure for the hundredth time that it is set to loud and put it back into my pocket. I let out a deep breath and look out to where the sun is getting ready to set.

"We had a good day. We had a great day, honestly, and then this happens. Seems like every time we get to a good place, one of us either says something to take it down a few pegs or something happens that edges us apart."

"You always find your way back together, though."

"I know," I say. "It's just exhausting. Why can't things just be simple and easy?"

"Because life itself is an exhausting experience, El."

"I leave at the end of May by the way."

I feel Ethan's eyes glance over to me and back towards the water.

"Have you talked to him about going yet?"

"No," I say. "I know I won't be there long term, though. I don't want to be. I want the experience, but I gotta come back here. My life is here."

"You still need to ask him to go with you, El."

"I know. Just haven't found a good time to ask him. Especially now."

"Ask him during sex," he says, laughing. "He'll say whatever you want him to then."

"Thought about it," I say.

"I have no doubt he'll go."

"I don't either. I don't know why I haven't asked him yet. I think I feel selfish asking him I guess."

"It's not selfish wanting the love of your life to be with you as you experience new and exciting things in your life."

"Still feels like I'm asking a lot out of him."

"When things calm down," he says, "ask him. If you don't ask him soon then I'm going to ask him myself for you."

"You still talking to that guy?"

"Yeah," he says. "We finally did it. It was damn good, too. It was nice fucking for pleasure for once and not to feel something."

"Fucking for pleasure is nice, I agree."

"He's a good guy," he says. He looks from the water to the sidewalk where couples are walking hand in hand down the sidewalk.

"But?"

"What?" he says.

"What's wrong with him?"

"Nothing's wrong with him. It's me."

"There's nothing wrong with you," I say.

"It's just weird for me," he says. "I've never met someone who treated me like this. He really cares about me."

"Do you not like him as well?"

"I do," he says. "I don't know. It's just new. I want you to meet him. Dinner in a few weeks with you and William."

"I can't wait," I say, smiling. "I've been waiting to meet someone that isn't dumb as a box of rocks."

"I know," he says. "I'm sorry about Paul. Well, mostly about Ricky."

"He was fine," I say. "Just the opposite of what I wanted at the time."

"But," he says, smiling, "in a way, you never would have met Will if it wasn't for me. You met him that night because of our shitty double date. So, you're welcome I guess."

I grab his shoulder and hug him into me.

"Thank you, Ethan. You truly did me a solid that night by making me have a terrible night that turned into a great one."

"I try, I try."

My phone dings and I immediately dig into my pocket to get it out.

***Everything's fine. Talk later.***

"That him?"

"Yeah," I say. "Said everything's fine and we'll talk later."

"Good."

"I guess."

"Maybe it has something to do with his ex," he says.

"What do you mean?"

"Didn't he die in a car crash?"

I close my eyes and throw my head back. My thoughts cease completely and I look over at Ethan who looks confused as hell as to what is going on. How could I ***not*** remember the fact that Evan died in a car crash?

"Horribly," I say. "It really fucked Will up."

"Well," he says, raising his eyebrows, "that probably explains why he was weird."

"I'm an idiot," I say. "That and Lydia is going to be having her baby soon, so I'm sure that crossed his mind, too."

I text him back and put my phone back in my pocket.

"You want me to take you back home?"

"I don't know," I say. "He needs some space right now, but I don't want him to think that I don't care."

"I'm sure he'd like you being there when he got home."

"I just hope he's OK."

"I'm sure he is," he says.

"No," I say, "I mean, his ex dying really did a number on him. The anniversary is actually coming up either this week or next." I close my eyes again, bring my knees in close to my chest and rest my head on them. "I hope he doesn't shut down on me, Ethan."

"If anyone can bring him out of it, it's you," he says.

I look up to him and rest my head to the side.

"I know we were friends when everything happened to me, but if I hadn't had you helping me through things with Rick, I wouldn't be here. Even if he does shut down, you can bring him out of it. He's survived it all once, right?"

"I've never loved anyone like I do him," I say, tearing up. I wipe my nose and loosen the hold on my knees. "I'm terrified I'm going to lose him and I don't know why. With London and now this."

Ethan wraps his arm around me and I rest my head on his shoulder. "It's fine. It's all going to be fine."

# Chapter Sixteen

Will

IT'S MIDNIGHT WHEN I FINALLY get home from the hospital and the anxiety has worn off to the point where I can think clearly.

I walk in the door and see Elliot lying on the couch asleep. I set my wallet and keys down on the table and make my way over to the couch. Elliot is curled in a position that looks extremely uncomfortable and I laugh because his mouth is wide open and he is snoring louder than I've ever heard him snore before.

I sit down on the couch where there is room and accidentally sit on his foot. His snoring stops and he slowly wakes up and scoots back into a sitting position where he was laying down.

He looks at me with one eye closed and says," Hey, babe."

"Hey," I say. He leans into me and lays his head against my shoulder.

"You OK?"

"Yeah," I say. "Sorry for the way I left."

"It's OK," he says. I run my fingers through his hair and look over to the TV.

"They're OK?"

"Yeah, just bruised up a bit. Baby is fine, too."

"What happened?" he asks.

"They were on the interstate and a car side-swiped them. Fucker was going way too fast and they veered off the road into the guardrail. Abbey is perfectly fine, just shaken. Lydia has some cuts and her arm is messed up, but they're OK. It's all OK."

Elliot doesn't say anything and I look down to see if he fell back asleep, but his eyes are on the TV.

"The first thing I thought about when I got the call was when I got the call about Evan. That's why I left the way I did. I don't know how to handle stuff like this."

"I'm glad you are OK," he says.

"I don't remember driving to the hospital. I knew they were fine because he said they were fine on the phone, but when I got the call about Evan, they had the wrong info and told his mom that he was doing fine too en route to the hospital, but then, yeah."

"I wasn't sure whether I should go home or not, so I stayed and waited for you. Well I tried, but fell asleep apparently."

"I'm glad you're here," I say. "You keep me grounded."

"I just want you to know how much I love you," he says. "Finding you has been the best thing that's ever happened to me. Without you, I wouldn't be doing a lot of the things I'm doing now."

"I love you too, El."

I get up off the couch and make my way to the kitchen. I haven't eaten since this morning and I am starving.

"I went and ate with Ethan earlier. I got the fish you like for you. You'll just have to warm it up."

I open up the fridge and see the food from one of my favorite restaurants and my mouth starts to water. I heat it all up in the microwave and make my way back to the couch.

"Why are you so good to me?" I ask him, planting a kiss on his lips.

"You deserve it," he says.

Elliot falls back asleep quickly and I finish my food. I sit there motionless, the TV screen a blur even though my eyes are fixated on it, and think about everything that's happened today.

The day started off good with lunch and sex and happiness and ended with me reliving a moment a never wanted to experience again and wondering if my sister and niece were going to leave this world just like Evan did.

Elliot's head cocks to the right in my lap and it startles me out of my daze. I look down at his face and my eyes start to water. I smooth away some stray hairs off his face and take a deep breath - exhaling all the stress of the day and letting the negative energy leave my body in whatever way it can.

The two-year anniversary of Evan's death is this week and last year when I went and saw him, too many emotions hit me at once and I couldn't handle it just like the day he died. I also didn't have Elliot last year, though, either.

I look down at his beautiful face and a wave of thankfulness courses through me. I think about him leaving for London and wonder if he is going to ask me to go with him or not. I figured he already would have, but I'm starting to wonder if he even wants me to. I know he loves me, but maybe his new opportunities outweigh that love. I was just relived when he told me that he wasn't going to be over there long-term.

Even if he doesn't ask me, I can wait for him to get back. I can visit and text and video chat if that means keeping one of the best things about my life in my life and my happiness in check.

***

"So what time do you want to go?" Lydia asks me across the table.

"I don't know," I say, fixing Abbey's ponytail. I fix it and she turns to me and puts out her hand to me like a high-five. I look over to Lydia and laugh and give her a high-five back and she giggles.

"That's new," I say, laughing.

"She's learning all sorts of new things lately," she says. "She's been saying the f word a lot here lately."

"Fun?"

"Yes," she says, rolling her eyes. "No, I wish she was saying fun."

"I cussed a lot when I was younger, too."

"I guess," she says. "I just don't want it to become a habit. It doesn't embarrass me or anything, but she already has enough words to learn and that one isn't needed."

"You don't have to go with me if you don't want to," I say.

"I don't mind," she says. "We can at least drive you there and you can have your time with him."

"We can go once we leave here then," I say. "It won't be like last year, I promise."

"I know it won't," she says.

"How's your arm doing?" I say, pointing my fork towards it.

"It's fine," she says. "Just sore. Still wish I knew who the fucker was that hit me."

"And you wonder why she is saying that," I say. "And the baby hasn't acted up?"

"No," she says, "he's fine. I've been driving slower since I got out of the hospital. I check the rearview mirror a hundred times on Abbey. I'm just overly hesitant. Just glad we're OK."

"Me too," I say.

Lydia looks at Abbey and brings her hand to her mouth as she looks out the window of the restaurant. I see her eyes start to moisten and she wipes the bottom of her eye with her finger.

"You OK?"

"Yeah," she says. "It's just a lot to deal with lately. The wreck and the baby will be here within the next week or so I'm guessing and Greg is still working like crazy. I just don't know if I can raise another kid on my own again."

"You won't be alone," I say. "You'll always have me."

"I know," she says.

We leave the restaurant and make our way to the cemetery. I've only been to his site twice: the funeral and the one-year anniversary. I have the path from the road to his grave memorized in my mind and I don't even remember making my way there in either instance.

Along the way, I see a flower shop and flag it down to Lydia. She pulls over and parks while I walk in and get some roses.

I get back in the car and she says, "Roses?"

"They were always his favorite."

The rest of the drive there is nothing but silence, aside from the kid music on the radio for Abbey. The sun has hidden itself under the clouds and the wind has picked up as I get out of the car and make my way up the cemetery path.

My eyes stay focused on the brick-laid path as I walk up and I don't veer my vision left or right as I pass different people.

As I get closer to Evan's gravesite, I look up and see someone standing above his grave. My movements slow as I get closer and I realize who it probably is that is standing there.

I get two graves away and he says, "Will?"

"Do I know you?"

"No," he says. "Sorry, my name's Drew. I used to know him."

I look into Drew's eyes and feel nothing. The thought that he is Elliot's ex doesn't cross my mind, but instead, I think about the fact that he knew Evan before I ever did.

"We used to—"

"You grew up together," I say, cutting him off. "Yeah, I know about you." I extend my hand and he shakes it. He rubs his right eye and sniffs and looks from the gravestone to the trees behind it.

"He was a great person," he says. "I know we weren't blood, but he was my brother. He was family. I miss him."

"He was amazing," I say.

"I'm gonna go," he says. "I've been here for awhile. Time for me to go."

He turns and moves past me towards the brick path.

"Thank you," I say. He turns around and looks at me. "I'm sure it means a lot to him that you came."

"Take care, Will."

He makes his way down the path and I turn back around to Evan's gravestone. I scratch my temple and lay the roses down in front of where his birth year is. I sit myself crossed-legged in front of the stone and pull up a piece of grass and throw it to the side.

"Hey," I say, wiping my nose. "A lot's happened since last year. I'm doing better. I still miss you, though. Everyday."

I reposition the roses and look up at the sky.

"I met someone new. His name is Elliot and he's been a life savior. I was feeling like I was betraying you in finding someone new, but I know now it had to happen. I wonder sometimes if someone up there with you pushed him my way or if you did. Lydia's doing good. She was in a wreck the other day. Brought back some things, but I'm OK. And she's having another baby, so that's exciting. Told her she needs to name it Will, but I doubt she will."

I see a smudge of dirt towards the bottom of the stone and wipe it away with my thumb.

"I think I'm still going to stick to once a year," I say. "If you're listening then you're always listening and it's just easier this way. I hope you understand."

My phone dings and I pull it out of my pocket.

***I'll pick you up around 6.***

I reply to Elliot and put the phone back in my pocket. I move my legs, bringing one into my chest, and lean on one knee, resting my head on the top.

"I could tell you all the things that have happened, but it's not important. Just know that…I'm happy. I never thought I would be after everything, but I think I've finally reached a good place. I've stopped having panic attacks at least and I don't have flashbacks like I did. I owe a lot to Elliot for that. He's helped me in ways that I'll never be able to thank him for or express to him. That friend of yours, Drew, I wish I could've known him. So many things about your younger years that you were probably too embarrassed to tell me about; so many stories I wish I could've heard about you."

I get off the grass and put my hands in my pockets.

"I love you, Evan. I always will. I hope wherever you are that you're happy, too. I hope me moving on isn't a bad thing and that I'm doing the right thing. I hope I stay happy in spite of everything. I hope you know that you'll never leave my heart even if Elliot has a place in it now."

I turn around and make my way back to the brick path. A heavy breath leaves my mouth and I feel relief. I know I can think about him now without having a breakdown and the thought brings me a calm I haven't experienced in a while.

"Everything OK?" Lydia asks me as I shut the car door closed.

I look over to her and smile and say, "Everything's OK."

***

"So," I say to Elliot across the table from me, "I met Drew."

Elliot's face remains unchanged and he says," He was there?"

"Yeah. Was getting ready to leave once I got there."

"He say anything?"

"Not really," I say. "Is it weird that all I wanted to do was ask him about Evan when he was younger?"

"No," he says. "Makes sense."

"He seemed nice, I guess."

"He's not a bad guy," he says.

"How was your day?"

"Boring," he says. "I took a nap and finished a book I was reading."

"You sure you'll be able to handle working again?"

"I don't know," he says. "Not having as many naps isn't going to be easy for me. Slumming it the past few weeks has been pretty nice really."

"Well," I say, "that's what lunch breaks are for."

"One way or another, I'll find a way to have a nap or two."

He smiles and goes back to his food.

"So, there's something I've been meaning to ask you and I know today isn't the greatest day to ask, but it's just a nonstop thought in my head at this point and I got to get it out."

I raise my eyebrows at him and say, "Alright."

"I know it's asking a lot, but I want you to come to London with me. If not it's OK, but I just want you there."

"I—"

"I'm sorry," he says, putting down his fork. "I wouldn't expect you to uproot everything to—"

"Elliot," I say, smiling, "I would like nothing more then to go to London with you."

His eyes widen and he says, "For real?"

"Well, why wouldn't I?"

"I don't know," he says. "That's just a lot for me to ask of you and—"

"I'd do anything for you," I say. "Even move to a different country for awhile."

"It's only temporary."

"I know."

"I'll support you," he says. "Don't feel like you have to have something lined up."

"I'm sure I can work something out with them here."

"Cool," he says. "If not, though, it's—"

"Honestly," I say, "I've been wondering if you were even going to ask me. If you hadn't, it would've been fine, but I'm glad you did. Another stresser gone."

"I know," he says. "I don't know why I haven't until now. Think I was afraid to ask that much of you. I didn't want to make you feel like you had to or something. I don't know."

"I need to update my passport."

"I haven't even thought about that," he says.

"Kind of important."

"I'll have to call them tomorrow and tell them you're coming with me. They're handling all my documentation and stuff."

He looks into my eyes and his face grows serious.

"You're sure you want to go? If you really don't it won't change anything between us."

"I'm sure."

"Okay," he says.

I smile up at him and say, "Okay."

"I love you," he says.

"Same."

"I'm also paying for this tonight so don't try and stop me," he says.

"I guess I'm just have to pay you back somehow then, won't I?"

A grin flashes across his face and he bites his bottom lip.

"Like your laundry or something," I say, focusing back on my food.

"My thoughts exactly," he says, laughing.

# Chapter Seventeen

Elliot

"WHAT TIME IS dinner with Ethan?" Will asks me from the kitchen.

"Nine I think."

"Has he told you anything about this Cody guy?"

"Just that he likes him," I say. "Which that says a lot to be honest."

"Well," he says, "it's good he's found someone. Hopefully he's a good guy."

"The dinner is a test I think."

"What?" he asks.

"An approval thing."

"Well this is the first guy he's dated since the bad one, right?"

"This is the first guy he has dated in general for awhile now. The other guys were just hookups and ways to relieve whatever was bothering him."

"I'm sure it will be a nice night."

"Hopefully," I say.

Will makes his way into the living room and sits down next to me on the couch.

"Only a few more weeks," he says.

"I know."

"It's gonna be exciting, Elliot."

"I know," I say. "Sorry, I don't mean to not seem enthused. It's just a lot of changes and in the past, change this fast hasn't always been great for me."

"Well," he says, "you have me going through the changes with you. It will be fun. I'm excited to be honest."

"Did you get everything figured out with work then?"

"Yeah," he says. "I can do most of it from over there now that we have most of the positions filled and everything. I can do conference calls via web cam. There are a couple big events this summer that I'll have to fly back for, but it will only be a day or two out of the week, so it will be fine."

"Well, maybe we'll get over there and hate London and we'll want to move back immediately."

"Maybe," he says, "but I highly doubt it, so perk up. It will be nice to visit a new country that isn't full of depressing places and people. Not that I didn't love every moment I spent at those places, but this will be nice regardless."

"I'm glad you're coming," I say. I bury my head into his shoulder and he wraps his arm around me.

"Lydia is about ready to have that baby any minute now," he says, picking his phone up and reading a text message from her. "I might have to leave early."

"I know," I say. "It's OK. I can't wait to see him."

"They still haven't picked out a name."

"Maybe they're going to surprise you by naming him after you," I say.

"I doubt it," he says. "Still think a middle name would be nice, though."

"Is Abbey excited?"

"As excited as she can be," he says. "I don't think she really knows what is going on fully. Just that her mom has gotten fatter."

"I'm surprised she isn't bigger, honestly," I say.

"I know. When she had Abbey she was huge."

"Were you there when she had Abbey?"

"Yeah," he says. "Our parents were never the greatest, so I was the only one was there for her. Greg was there of course. He's there now or I would be."

"Think he'll slow down on working now that she's excepting this one?"

"No," he says. "But that's OK, she'll have me."

"And me," I say. He leans over and plants a kiss on my lips.

"I love you," he says.

"Same."

***

"So, what made you become a nurse?" I ask Cody across the table from me.

Cody is taller than Ethan and a lot more muscular than Ethan, which Ethan must love. Cody's arms are bigger than Ethan's thighs and I could only imagine the things he's had those arms do.

"My mom was one," he says, smiling. "My freshman year in college I was trying to figure what I wanted to do and she got really sick and I ended up dropping out and taking care of her. Once she passed, I knew what I wanted to do and be."

"I'm sorry," I say. "That's an amazing story, though."

"He's damn good at it, too," Ethan says beside him.

"I'm lucky," Cody says. "It might not seem like it, because of the reasons I figured out what I wanted to do, but it helped me find my passion and help people in general. She would've liked the fact that I became one."

"Did you go to the university here for nursing?" Will asks Cody.

"Yeah, just graduated a few years ago this June."

"I'm pretty sure I taught you in a comp class."

"I think you did," he says, laughing. "Professor Everett, right? To be perfectly honest, I hated that class. Not because of you, you were a great teacher, but English was never one of my favorite things."

"Very few people end up loving it, so I understand."

"When are you guys leaving by the way?" Ethan asks.

"Two weeks from now," I say. "Next weekend I have that trip with Hadley and then the weekend after that we're going."

"Are you excited?" Cody asks me.

"Yeah," I say looking over to Will. "I mean, mostly. Just hard leaving everything here behind I guess."

"We'll be here when you get back," Ethan says.

"I know," I say.

"Honestly," Will says, "I'm guessing the next few months will fly by. We'll be back before you know it."

"I've always wanted to visit London," Cody says. "Maybe I'll come with Ethan to visit you guys one weekend this summer."

"Who said I was going to visit them?" Ethan says. "My god that's a lot of money flying over there and back."

"Am I not worth it?" I ask him.

"Of course, dear friend," he says.

"We'll be there, don't worry," Cody says, laughing.

Ethan looks over to Cody and a huge grin comes across his face. I haven't seen a grin like that on his face in years and it warms me. He looks over to me and immediately glares as he sees me smiling.

"Isn't your sister having her baby soon, Will?" Ethan says.

"Any minute now, yeah," he says. "I told her to let me know once she starts actually having him and I'll come over."

"Have they figured out a name for him yet?" Ethan asks.

"No," Will says. "They were that way with Abbey too though, so it will probably be a few days before they decide on something."

"Do you have any siblings, Cody?" I ask.

"I have an older brother," he says. "He lives in Texas. Moved away once he graduated high school. I talk to him sometimes, but he hasn't been a part of my life really."

Ethan makes eye contact with me and very slowly shakes his head from side to side where Cody can't notice. Cody doesn't seem bothered by the question, but I'm guessing there is more to it that Ethan knows about, so he changes the subject.

"Where are you and my sister going anyway?"

"Pittsburgh," I say. "She has her seminar Saturday and she's speaking for something and then the rest of the weekend we're just going to sight-see and enjoy the city."

"I couldn't imagine working in law enforcement," Cody says. "It's hard enough seeing some of the people that come in from things that happen around the city. I wouldn't want to actually be there in the thick of it all."

"I wish she'd do something else," Ethan says.

"She never will," I say.

"I know," he says. "That will be fun, though, I guess. It's a nice city."

"They have a nice campus there, too," Will says.

"It will be nice to get away," I say. "Mainly spend some time with her alone since I'm leaving soon."

"I think she's the most upset out of all of us," Ethan says. "She's beyond happy for you, but you know how close you guys are."

"I know," I say.

An hour passes and we all finish our food. Ethan's happiness doesn't waver and Cody sends nothing but positive vibes towards me and Will.

Will's phone dings and I see the screen brighten up on his lap as he looks down at it.

He looks over at me and smiles and says, "It's time."

"I'll go with you," I say.

"No," he says, "it's fine. You—"

"We have to go anyway," Ethan says. "Cody has to work a shift in an hour and I'd like to spend a second with him before he leaves."

I smile at Will and he says, "Okay."

"It was really nice meeting you, Cody," I say as Will and I make our ways out of the booth.

"You guys, too," he says, shaking my hand. "I hope everything goes well over there. And congratulations on the new baby."

"Thank you," Will says, shaking his hand as well.

Ethan gives Will a hug and stops me as Will and Cody make their way outside.

"So?"

"He's really nice," I say. "And very nice to look at."

"Those arms, right?"

I smile at him and he pulls me in for a hug.

"Make sure I see you before you go," he says.

"Of course, bud," I say.

We make our way outside and Will is waiting by the car talking to Cody. Cody waves goodbye to us as he makes his way back to Ethan. Will gets in the car and I get in seconds after.

"Let's go see Will Jr," I say as Will looks over to me and smiles.

***

We get to the hospital and find Lydia's room, but they won't let us back to see her.

"I'm her brother," Will says, leaning on the counter.

"Sir," the woman behind the counter says, "we haven't gotten an update on her yet, so I can't let you back to her room."

"Well, can you check right now and then you'll know?"

"Sir—"

"Is there someone who ***could*** find out for me instead?"

"Will," I hear a man say behind us. It must be Greg. He's wearing a cap and gown and he has a huge smile on his face.

"Did she have it?"

"Yeah," he says, coming to Will for a hug. Will looks at me and rolls his eyes and I laugh a little as they stand there celebrating the new baby.

"Can we go see her?"

"Yeah, he says. "Come on."

Will looks at the woman at the counter again and smiles.

"Got it," he says, "but thanks anyway."

She smiles back and watches us as we make our way back to Lydia's room.

We make our way down a few hallways and several rooms until finally we walk in to see Lydia holding a beautiful baby boy.

"He's so beautiful," Will says, walking over to her.

He kisses her on top of her head and touches the baby's finger as he kneels down closer to it. Abbey runs over to me and gives me a huge hug as I sit down in one of the chairs to the side of the room.

"Did you name him?" Will says, not taking his eyes off the baby.

Lydia looks over at me and back to Will and says, "We did."

Will looks up to her and says, "And?"

"Evan Alexander Morgan."

Will looks over at me and his eyes instantly start to water. He looks back down to the baby and smiles through the tears.

"That's even better than my name," he says, laughing. "Thank you."

"How's Elliot doing tonight?" Lydia asks me.

"He's doing good," I say, smiling. "Kind of exhausted, but I'm sure you win on that one."

"Oh, yes," she says, laying her head back. "Pushing him out has drained me of all my energy for awhile I'd say. Way more energy than Abbey, I swear."

She looks over to Will and says, "Did you guys at least get to finish dinner?"

"You started having him just in time," he says. "Literally perfect timing."

Will picks him up and brings him over to me. I've never held a baby before or really been around one in general since I've had no siblings and don't have a lot of family. He sits down beside me and Abbey touches the baby's face gently and laughs.

"Do you want to hold him?" Will asks me.

I don't say anything and instead just hold out my hands. Will doesn't notice my un-comfortableness in the moment and gently sets him in my arms. A warmth runs through me like I've never experienced before and I get lost in the baby's features.

The idea that something this small will one day grow into something so big is beautiful, and magical even, and it's beyond hard to explain how complex the idea is. I've never really thought about kids in a serious way, but instead have liked the idea in a general sense.

I know Will wants kids because we've talked about it, but also because of the way he reacted when he met this one. My mind wanders quickly to us having kids again and having vacations at the beach and building sandcastles and moving away from the waves. I know in this moment that a life with Will is more than anything I could have ever imagined and I wonder if he wants the same things as badly as I do.

I hand the baby back to Will and Will hands him back to Lydia.

"I think we're going to go," Will says to her. "Let you get some rest."

"Okay," she says. "Thanks for coming, baby brother."

"I'll be back tomorrow to see how you're doing. I love you.

"Love you too, Will," she says. "Bye, Elliot."

"Bye," I say. "Bye, Abbey."

"Bye," she says, snickering.

Will shakes Greg's hand and we wave goodbye as we make our way out of the room and down the hallways back to the waiting room. As we makes our way past the nurses station again, the woman we were talking to earlier doesn't even look up from her desk as we walk by and Will is so lost in thought that he doesn't notice me laughing to myself about the situation.

We get to the car and Will doesn't start the car as I shut my door and buckle my seat belt. He rests his hands on the steering wheel and looks straight ahead as he seems to be lost in his own thoughts.

"You alright?" I ask him.

"Yeah," he says. "Just holding the baby…I realized that things do get better. Things have gotten better in my life and there's a lot of reasons why, but you're the main reason and I'm just beyond thrilled to start our life together."

He looks over to me and kisses me as he starts the car. He puts on his seat belt and laughs.

"This has been a good day," he says.

# Chapter Eighteen

Will

SEEING THE BABY GOT ME thinking about all the wonderful things I have now, but also about all of the wonderful things that I don't have but want.

When I look at Elliot, I see kids and marriage and a dog and a picket fence and a pool. All I can do is wonder if Elliot wants the same things, too.

I never thought I would even want to get married again after Evan, but moving on has only made the thought torment me every time I'm around Elliot or thinking about Elliot in general since I held the baby.

Lydia is back home with the baby and doing fine, so I told her I would come over and see her today. On my way there, I see a jewelry store along the highway and I immediately swerve into the next lane and pull into the parking lot.

My hands are rested on the steering wheel and the car is still on and all I can think about is whether or not I should go in. Proposing to Elliot is something that terrifies me more than anything because I don't know where he is completely at with us. I know he loves me and wants to be with me, but marriage is a whole other layer that he may or may not be ready for.

I get out of the car and go inside. There's no one around besides the guy behind the register, so he instantly comes to me and asks, "What can I help you with today?"

"I'm looking for engagement rings," I say.

"Oh," he says. "Wonderful! Right this way."

"Do you have an idea of what she would want?"

"Oh," I say, "it's actually a he and I really just want a matching set I guess."

The guy smiles and walks towards the other rings that are two cases down.

"I'm not sure what you're looking to spend," he says. "Here's our newest collection. As you move down this way they'll get cheaper and cheaper. I'll let you look and just get me if you see something you like or if you have any questions in general."

Every ring I look at, I imagine on Elliot and I's fingers and I don't like any of them. When I finally set my eyes on one set I like, the price tag makes me gag a tad. It's affordable, but I'm not sure if getting them will be beneficial and I don't want to waste the time.

I don't move from the case for some time and the worker eventually makes his way back over to see what I'm looking at.

"You want to try it on?" he asks.

I set my finger out and he puts the ring on it. A shiver runs through me and I smile as thoughts of Elliot and I, hand and hand getting married, flash through my mind. I realize that the only problem is that I don't know the size of Elliot's finger and the thoughts quickly disappear.

"Something wrong?" he says.

"I just have no idea what size his fingers are to be honest," I say.

"That's OK," he says. "You could still get them and let us know later today what size it is."

"If I brought you in a random ring of his, like a class ring or something, would that work? I just want to make sure it's the right fit."

I remember that Elliot has a class ring stowed away in a box with a bunch of random school things he saved years ago.

"Yep," he says.

I don't say anything and continue to look at the ring.

"So," he says, "what's it gonna be?"

***

"You were supposed to be here an hour ago," Lydia says as I walk through the front door.

"I know," I say. "I forgot something and had to run back to the apartment once I was mostly here. Then I had to get gas and, yeah."

Lydia doesn't say anything more and walks over to the kitchen table where Abbey is eating lunch.

"Where's the baby?" I ask her.

"In his crib," she says. "He literally just fell asleep about ten minutes ago. I was hoping you'd be here before that because I knew it was gonna happen."

"It's OK," I say. "How are you doing?"

"Fine," she says. "He's been surprisingly good. Doesn't cry a whole lot. The opposite of Abbey when she was born."

"Has Greg been home more?"

"He took yesterday off," she says. "We actually talked when I left the hospital. I told him I wasn't doing all of this on my own and he didn't realize how he basically hasn't been here to see Abbey grow up. He's going to try."

"That's good," I say.

"I'm so tired," she says. "He doesn't cry a whole lot, but when he does cry it's at night and I don't get to sleep and then I wake up and have Abbey and it's just a constant cycle."

"Well, Elliot is leaving for the weekend. I can come stay if you want. I'll take care of them while you sleep. That or I can take Abbey for the weekend."

"That would be great, baby brother."

I look out the kitchen window and rest my chin on my hand as I watch Lydia's neighbors across the street play with their kids. I let out a deep breath and zone back in to Lydia who's standing by the entrance to the kitchen with her arms crossed.

"What's up?" she asks me.

"Nothing," I say. "Just ever since you had him, I've been thinking a lot about me and Elliot and if we'll ever have all this."

"Why wouldn't you?"

"I don't know," I say. "Last time I was close to having it all, it was taken away from me in an instant."

"You're overthinking, like usual."

"I know."

"Where's he going anyway?"

"Pittsburgh with his friend for something for her work."

"And then you guys are leaving the week after, right?"

"Yeah," I say. "Are you sure it's OK if I go? If you need me here then I won't."

"William," she says, "I'm fine. I've done this before. And my husband has finally grown a set and is gonna step up and do his job so it will all be fine."

"Okay."

"You need to perk up," she says. "You're going to London in a week to spend the summer with a guy who is madly in love with you. What's wrong?"

"Just feeling kind of blah today I guess."

"Are you guys doing anything special before he leaves?"

"Dinner," I say.

I hear a faint cry a few rooms over and I see Lydia roll her eyes as she turns to the wall and mimics slamming her head into it.

"Let me go get him," I say, laughing.

I make my way down the hallway into the baby's room and make my way to the crib. I look over the side of the crib and see the baby's beautiful blue eyes looking up at me as he slowly squirms back and forth with his hands in front of his face.

A small smile flashes across his face as he makes eye contact with me, and a warmth runs through my body like no other. I hear Lydia walk in the room as the door creaks open slowly, but my eyes don't move from the baby's face.

"He really is beautiful," I say.

"He is," she says, coming up behind me and rubbing my shoulder.

"Abbey was beautiful when she was born too, but this is different."

"You didn't want one of your own when Abbey was born is why."

I look over to her and nod my head.

"I didn't realize it until the other night at the hospital," I say. "We got back in the car and it just hit me that this is what I wanted. I want a family and a house and all the things that make life worth living. I'm finally at a good place emotionally and I have a job I love more than anything and I have Elliot which has changed me in only good ways."

"Maybe you should look into making it all a reality then, Will."

"I still can't believe you named him Evan," I say, laughing. "It makes him even more beautiful."

"As soon as I found out I was pregnant," she says, "I knew I wanted a part of him to stay with me in a way, too. Evan meant a lot to me, too. He treated you the way you deserved to be treated and I loved him for that. Growing up, I never thought you'd let someone in the way you did him. Dad leaving us had a bigger effect on you than it did me and I'm just glad it didn't ruin your trust in people completely."

"He wasn't worth giving up anything for," I say. "I realized that in college when I met Evan."

"I like Elliot, too," she says. "I'm sure he is thinking about the same things you are right now. Probably not as much because of all the other stuff he has going on, but I'm sure spending his life with you is a top priority."

***

"How's the baby?" Elliot asks me as we make our way back home from dinner.

"Adorable," I say. "He smiled at me today. It was cute."

"And Lydia's doing good?"

"Yeah. She's really tired. I told her I'd help her out this weekend while you were gone."

"Good," he says.

Silence fills the car as we get closer and closer to Elliot's apartment. Dinner was fine and we mainly talked about London and this weekend, but there was a hint of tension the whole time and it's because of me.

"You excited to get to spend some time with Hadley before you go?"

"Yeah," he says. "I haven't seen her since our dinner. She's been busy with work and I've been busy trying to get everything figured out before we leave. It'll be nice to have some fun with her."

"She has never been there either, has she?"

"No," he says. "She doesn't travel much in general. She's only going this weekend because it involves work, and even this she wasn't thrilled about."

We pull up to his apartment and I find a spot to park in a few cars up.

"You OK?" he says, unbuckling his seatbelt.

"No," I say.

He turns to his side and rests his hand on the back of my neck and says, "What is it?"

"I've just been thinking a lot lately about random shit."

"Like what?"

"Like babies," I say. "Babies and marriage and a dog and a family."

"Okay?"

"Ever since Lydia had the baby, everything has just been nonstop in my brain and I don't know what to do."

"Why are you freaking out about it?"

"I don't know," I say, letting out a deep breath.

"Do you not think I want those things too or—"

"I don't know that either. I hope you do."

"I do," he says, laughing.

"Okay," I say.

"Jesus," he says, "is this why you've been weird all night? I knew something was up when you kept staring at me without saying anything every time I looked up."

"I'm sorry," I say.

"It's OK," he says. "Let's go upstairs and have an actual conversation, yeah?"

We make our way upstairs and I walk directly to the bathroom and take a very long, held-in-all-day piss. I hear the TV turn on as I go to flush and I make my way back out to the living room. Elliot is sitting with his phone in his hand on the side of the couch and he looks up as I make my way to the couch beside him.

"Get it all out?"

"Yeah," I say, laughing.

I lay my head into his shoulder and he runs his fingers through my hair, waiting for me to say something.

"I don't want you to think I'm going crazy or something," I say. "These thoughts aren't bad ones. I mean, they are just overwhelming me. The thought of marriage again scares me."

"Why?"

"Because the last time I was close to being married, it was all taken away from me."

He stops rubbing my head for a second, but continues and says, "What else is scaring you?"

"I wouldn't even say it's scaring me," I say. "I just am overwhelmed with all these thoughts and I didn't realize how bad I wanted certain things."

"And you want those with me?"

"Of course," I say.

"Then why are you stressing out over all this for?"

"Because I'm not sure you want them, too," I say. "Well, I wasn't sure."

"Do I want kids right now?" he says. "No I don't. Do I want a house right now? Not right this minute. Do I want a dog right now? Yeah, but I can't get one."

I don't say anything and focus in on the TV waiting for him to continue.

"But do I want all of those things eventually?" he asks me. "Hell yes I do."

I laugh and lean off of him. I grab his mouth with my hand and plant my tongue firmly in his mouth. I swing my hips around and plant myself directly in front of him over his lap.

"I love you, Will," he says. "If you don't know that by now then I don't now what to tell you."

"I know," I say.

"When London's done," he says, "we'll talk more. Okay?"

"Okay."

"Can we go in the bedroom so I can have a reason to want to rush back here once the weekend is over?"

"Hell yes we can," I say, smiling.

# Chapter Nineteen

Elliot

"WHERE'S THE HOTEL at again?" I ask Hadley as we make our way out of the airport and into the first taxi we see.

"Close to the university," she says.

We keep our bags with us as we get in the backseat and Hadley tells the driver the address of the hotel. The airport is a good ways away from the city itself, so I take in everything around us as we make our way there. There's road construction everywhere I look as we make our way down the interstate and through each individual suburb.

"The city is a lot nicer," she says, looking over at me.

"I hope," I say, laughing.

"So," she says, looking out the window.

"So what?"

"So what's new with you? I haven't talked to you about anything for awhile."

"You shouldn't have slept on the plaaaaane."

"I know," she says, "I'm sorry. I left straight from work last night to your apartment."

"You couldn't take one night off, Had?"

"We've been busy," she says. "Plus I've been nervous for days about speaking, so it was just better that I keep myself busy."

"I forgot you don't like public speaking."

"Not in situations like this," she says. "I can handle talking to the people I work with, but talking to a room full of randoms just freaks me out. I'm really not looking forward to tomorrow."

"You'll be fine," I say, rubbing her shoulder.

"I know," she says. "I'm just so tired. I'm overworking myself and I know it has to stop."

"Maybe you should take a desk job," I say.

"Fuck that," she says.

"Well, what else are you going to do?"

"I don't know," she says. "Quit."

I laugh and look over at her. Her face is serious as she continues looking out the window.

"Wait," I say, "are you serious?"

"It's getting bad, El," she says. "I'm starting to wonder if it's all worth it. A guy in my unit, a really amazing guy with a wife and daughter, was shot a couple days ago en route to chase down this sick fucker we've been trying to catch for months. He's paralyzed, El. Got shot in the neck."

"You love what you do, though."

"I know," she says. "I just don't think I love it enough anymore to risk my life. I want other things and I'll never feel safe having those things as long as I'm doing this."

"Like what?"

"Like a husband and kids," she says.

"So doesn't Will."

She turns her attention toward me finally and smiles.

"Oh?" she says.

"His sister just had her baby boy and ever since then, he's just been weird and we finally talked about it last night. He wants kids and marriage and a dog and yeah."

"And you don't?"

"I do," I say. "Honestly, if he proposed to me right now I'd say yes in a heartbeat. I don't want kids right now. Not with us going to London."

"Well," she says, "it's not like they'd just be delivered to your door once you decide."

"I know that," I say, laughing. "He's just overwhelmed with all these thoughts and I'm not I guess and I wonder why."

"I mean, you've never really wanted those things really bad. You've never met someone that gave you reasons to want those things I mean."

"Yeah," I say, "and I do want those things with him, I really do. I just didn't really start thinking about it in a serious way until he brought it up."

"I wouldn't worry about it," she says. "I don't know why he is either. You love each other and both want those things so don't rush that shit. Just let it play it self out. Enjoy London first."

We eventually get to the hotel and as soon as we walk in the door, Hadley walks straight to the bed closest to the window and plops down onto the pillow.

"Just a quick nap," she says.

I laugh and realize that we'll be here the rest of the afternoon and night, but that's OK. I'm tired too and I'd rather just video chat with Will then go out.

I connect my phone to the hotel's wifi and make my way to the bathroom. I Facetime Will and look at my teeth in the mirror as it rings into him.

"You must not be doing anything exciting if you're already calling me," he says.

I laugh and look from the mirror back down to my phone.

"What are you doing?"

"Getting ready to take a shower," he says.

"Oh?"

"What?"

"Can I watch?"

He smiles at me and positions his phone against the mirror by the sink. The phone gives a perfect view of the shower and I realize that he's actually going to let me watch him take one.

"I wasn't serious," I say, laughing.

He comes back into view and I see that he is now in just his underwear and a plain white t-shirt.

"Where's Hadley?" he says.

"Sleeping," I say. "She didn't sleep last night so she'll be out for awhile."

"Good," he says.

He opens the shower curtain and turns on the water. He feels it and adjusts the temperature of the water until he is satisfied and makes his way back towards me.

"Do you remember when we went to the beach and how I had taken a shower before I came out to the balcony?"

"Yeah," I say.

"I never told you why I was in there for so long."

I feel my pants tighten in the crotch and I unzip them as I say, "Were you thinking about me?"

He shoves his hand down his underwear, grabs his cock and says, "Yeah."

I bite my bottom lip and sit down on the side of the bathtub. He slowly takes his hand out of his underwear and touches his stomach as he takes his shirt off. I imagine myself on my knees in front of him, licking down his stomach, as my tongue makes its way over every ridge of his abs.

He moves back closer to the shower and slowly scoots his underwear down his thighs until they drop to the floor. His cock springs to life once he un-cages it and it swings from side to side quickly before he grabs hold of it with his right hand.

He moves his left hand up and down his stomach as he makes his way to his nipples and pulls at them slowly. He jerks himself back and forth as he opens the shower curtain and steps inside. He leans back against the shower wall as I take off my pants and kick them to the side of the bathroom.

"How was your flight?" he says as he squirts some body wash into his loofa.

"What?" I say.

"Your flight," he says. "I know you hate flying."

"Please continue touching yourself and we can discuss this after."

He laughs and moves the loofa up and down his stomach until he circles it around to his ass. He runs it between his cheeks and my thoughts instantly imagine my cock between his cheeks as he moans and takes me deeper and deeper.

I look down and realize that I've been jerking off since I took off my pants and haven't realized it. I look back to my phone and see Will hanging up the loofa and massaging his body with his hands now.

He moans as he jerks himself back and forth and I close my eyes as I imagine myself there, in the shower with him, and softly moan myself. I open my eyes back up and see him coming out of the shower. He gets to the edge of the sink and pulls his cock back as he lets out a loud moan and comes all over his stomach. He takes his finger and moves it over his tip and then plants the hand back on his stomach as he rubs everything in.

I get off the side of the bathtub and get to the mirror just as I shoot and just miss the faucet and handles of the sink. I hear Will laughing as I turn and look back towards my phone and see him making his way back into the shower.

"I miss you," he says.

"I miss you more."

I grab my phone and put it back by the mirror as I wet a washcloth and clean up my mess.

"What time is your guys' thing tomorrow?"

"Early," I say. "I'm not going, though. She's nervous about it and she's leaving as soon as she speaks."

"Why is she nervous?"

"She's hated public speaking since college."

"It can be exhausting," he says.

"She also told me she is thinking about quitting law enforcement. Doesn't want to risk her life anymore. That and she wants a family she thinks."

"She needs a boyfriend first," he says, laughing.

"I know," I say. "She was serious, though, so I'd say she's looking."

"Well," he says, "good for her. She deserves to be happy. We all do."

"I feel like everybody is going through all these changes just as we are leaving for London."

"Like what?"

"Hadley wanting a family. Ethan actually dating instead of just fucking random guys."

"Me wanting a family, too," he says.

"Yeah," I say.

"I mean, at least it's good changes and not bad ones. We could all be turning to drugs or something."

"That we could," I say. "I'm gonna get off here. I'm starving so I'm going to try and find something within walking distance."

"Well," he says, "at least you're in the city I guess. Plenty of options."

"I love you."

"Love you, El."

***

"Sorry I fell asleep last night," Hadley says as she walks inside the hotel room door.

"It's OK," I say. "I was tired, too. How did it go?"

"Fine," she says. "It wasn't as bad as I thought it would be. Honestly, I didn't think it would be bad in the first place. I just hate speaking in front of people."

"Did you already eat?"

"No," she says. "I didn't figure you would've already either, so I waited."

"You were correct," I say, smiling.

"I know you too well. What do you want?"

"I don't care," I say, moving to the TV stand. I grab my wallet and phone and stick them in my pockets.

"Do you want to chill first or what?"

"No," she says, making her way into the bathroom. "Just let me pee real quick and we'll go."

I sit on the edge of the bed and check my phone as I wait for her to finish. I check my email and see a message from my contact in London confirming that everything is fine for next week.

"Alright, let's go enjoy this beautiful fucking city while we can."

We eventually find ourselves at a local pizza place and I hand the waiter our menus as Hadley checks her face in a mirror in her purse.

"You look fine," I say.

"I know," she says. "New city, new dick. Ya know?"

"I don't see you meeting someone at this time of day."

"You never know, El. Good dick is always out there when you least expect it in my past experiences."

"Like that guy at the restaurant the last time I saw you?"

"He was ***very*** good dick," she says, laughing. "He kind of was what made me realize I wanted more. Not with him or anything, but I just realized that I missed feeling close to someone and getting it in in general. What happened the other day just kind of confirmed things for me that I need a change in my life."

"Well, it's good you're realizing it now."

"Yeah," she says. "I just don't know what I'll do. I thought about going back to school. I always liked the idea of psychology."

"You could be a therapist."

"I thought more like criminal profiler," she says. "I'd like to know what makes some of these fuckers the way they are. It fascinates me in a weird way."

"That's a lot of schooling."

"I know," she says. "Only have one life, though, so might as well make the most out of it."

"I hope everything goes well in London," I say. "I'm just kind of blah about it the past few days."

"You'll have Will. It'll be fine."

"I'm just going to miss you guys."

"We'll still be here when you get back," she says.

"What do you think of Cody by the way?"

"He's a nice guy," she says. "He must be something special if Ethan is changing his ways. I know it's weird for him, though."

"If I come back and they're married or something—"

"I highly doubt that," she says, laughing. "Ethan and marriage is like anal and going in dry: it just doesn't work out."

"I think if he did meet the right person it would become plausible."

"Did you know Rick was going to propose? Sick fucker. Ethan actually found the ring a few days before he left him. It's one of the things that made him realize he had to get out of it."

"Does he still live in the city?"

"No," she says. "I occasionally do something I'm not supposed to and run checks on him. Only way I feel like I know Ethan's somewhat safe."

"Well this guy seems like a good one," I say. "I guess we'll see."

"So would you rather Will propose to you or you propose to Will?"

I don't expect her question and instantly look at her with confusion.

"What?"

"Just random," I say.

"Seriously," she says, "which one would you prefer?"

"I don't know," I say. "Him asking me would be nice I guess. I don't ever see it happening, though."

"Why not?"

"Last time he was engaged his fiancée was killed."

"Okay," she says. "But did he propose to him or vice versa?"

"I have no idea to be honest. What does that have to do with anything?"

"It doesn't I guess," she says. "Nevermind. Well then you need to ask him."

"Let's go buy a ring and I'll get right on it."

"Alright," she says.

"I'm kidding," I say. "Will and I will get married when the time is right. I don't want to rush things like that just because the topic is on both of our minds. What if we go to London and something happens and he ends up hating me?"

"That's not going to happen," she says.

"But what—"

"Shut up, Elliot. That boy is yours. Until you both shall die, he is yours."

***

"You sure you're OK?"

"What do you mean?" I ask her as we make our way back to the airport.

"I know this whole marriage thing has your brain running around in circles."

"I'm fine," I say.

"Elliot," she says, "just remember, we get to choose who we love. Whether that person loves us back or not is not our choice. Will loves you. That's all you need to know."

"So wise," I say. She laughs and lays her head on my shoulder as we make our way down the interstate.

"God, I'm gonna miss you these next few months," she says. "I swear if you don't actually come back once the summer is over I'm going to be pissed."

"I will be," I say. "It will all work out. Everything will."

My phone dings and I look down at the screen and see a message from Will.

***Waiting patiently for your return.***

I smile and text him back.

***On our way to the airport now. I'll be back in your arms before the night is over.***

In this moment, I realize that everything will be OK. London will go smoothly and Will and I will fall even more in love as the months go on. Everything that is meant to happen will happen.

Meeting Will after one of the shitiest blind dates ever is the best thing to ever happen to me and when I get home tonight, I'm going to make sure he knows it.

# Chapter Twenty

Will

"SAM IS GOING TO DROP US OFF at the airport tomorrow by the way," Elliot says to me from the kitchen. He brings me a plate filled with pasta and bread and I give him a kiss as he hands it to me and sits down beside me on the couch.

"He coming home tonight?"

"I don't know," he says. "He's going on a double date with Ethan and Cody tonight so depending on how that goes, he may or may not get some much needed dick after."

I laugh and switch the TV to something that doesn't have a commercial playing.

"You have everything ready for tomorrow?"

"Do *you*?" I ask him, back smiling.

"I know," he says, "I know. I'm just nervous one of us is going to forget something."

"Whatever we forget we can just buy over there. Plus, it will be cool and new and different because it's in a different country. So all-in-all it will be worth leaving behind in the first place."

"Such the optimist, William," he says.

"I try," I say. "What all did you and Ethan do this morning?"

"We went last minute clothes shopping and had lunch. He hugged me and cried a little and said he was going to miss me. It was cute. He also said not to tell anyone he cried or he'd kick my ass."

"I won't tell," I say. "Probably."

"How was Lydia and the baby when you went over today?"

"Good," I say. "Greg has been helping out more like he said he was going to, which quite honestly surprises me, but I'm glad. She told me to be careful."

"Always the protective sister," he says, laughing.

"Abbey gave me a big hug before I left. She has no clue what's going on, though, so after awhile she'll miss me I figure."

"I've been thinking," he says.

"Alright?" I say with pasta between my lips.

"When we get back, assuming everything goes well which I have no doubt that it will, I think we should get a place together."

The pasta falls out of my mouth and my mouth turns into a grin as I turn towards him and put my plate on the coffee table.

"I think that would be a good idea."

"Good," he says.

"Like an apartment or—"

"A house," he says. "I want to get a house. I hate renting and Sam is wanting to find a new place anyway because of his new job and I know you hate renting, too."

"Okay," I say. I pick my plate back up and focus my attention back to the TV.

"Cool," he says. "So, a house then?"

I look at him with a mouthful of pasta and say, "Whatever you want, stud."

***

I brush my teeth and make my way back into Elliot's bedroom. Sam text Elliot and said he wasn't coming back tonight, so my first thought was that I had to try and make Elliot's eyes roll into the back of his head one last time before London.

"Tomorrow's going to be so stressful," he says as I make my back to the bed. I pull the covers back and get under them as Elliot scoots closer and lays his head on my chest.

"It will be fine," I say, taking off my shirt.

"I know, I'm so tired."

"That's too bad," I say.

"Why?" he asks me, laughing.

I flip him onto his back and say, "I was wanting to relieve you of some of this stress." I kiss my way from his mouth to his neck as I shove my hand down his underwear and grab hold of his cock.

He sits up and takes off his shirt and throws it across the room. I move myself overtop of him and position myself between his legs.

"I can't wait to have sex with you in a different country," he says, smiling up at me as I kiss my way from his neck and down his stomach. I slowly kiss my way from his stomach, down to his hip and I scoot his underwear off and throw them to the side of the bed.

He moans as I stick the tip of his cock in my mouth and lick it. I smile and take him deeper inside of me as I get on my knees and jerk myself off a little.

Elliot puts his hand in my hair and slowly moves my head up and down as I go down on him further and I let off myself and focus my hand between his cheeks. He takes his hands off my head and I let off him and make my way back to his mouth, pulling his body tighter into me. He reaches down and grabs my cock and jerks it back and forth as his thumb circles my tip.

He reaches over and gets some lube off the nightstand, squirts it in his palm and palms my cock and I let out a moan as he massages the tip of my cock. He arches his legs back and rubs the rest between his cheeks as he bites his bottom lip and pulls me closer to him.

He wraps his legs around me and locks me in as I lift his left leg and sit it on my shoulder, slowly shoving myself into him. He tightens and then loosens as I move in and out of him slowly. As he gets comfortable, I speed up until my full length is inside him.

"Oh, fuck," he says as I thrust my hips forward into him. I move his other leg onto my other shoulder as I reposition my stance and shove into him faster. The pleasure is unrelenting as my thighs smack into his.

I can feel myself close to coming as he arches his back and grabs both of my ass cheeks and pulls me deeper into him with each thrust.

"Oh, fuck," he says again as I take my hand and jerk him back and forth, faster and faster the closer I get to coming.

"I'm gonna come," I say as I pull out and position myself over his chest.

Elliot shoots onto his stomach right before I do and a smile flashes across his face as he sits up and sticks my cock in his mouth. I unload into his mouth and nearly pass out from the pleasure as I slink over onto my back and he rests his head on my chest.

"This is gonna be a good summer," he says.

"I can't fucking wait."

***

"How was your date?" Elliot asks Sam at breakfast the next morning.

"Very nice," he says, smiling. "It was nice to get out."

"You going to go see him again?" I ask.

"Nah," he says. "It was a nice date. Nothing more."

"That's too bad," Elliot says.

"It's fine, El. I can't believe you guys are leaving me."

Elliot pats him on the shoulder and says, "I know, buddy. You'll just have to come visit us."

"How's the new job going?" I ask.

"Good," he says. "I love it, honestly. I'm finally at that place in my life where I feel mostly fulfilled."

"We all are I think," Elliot says. "Even Hadley is figuring out what she wants and Ethan has Cody now."

"Cody is a cool guy," Sam says. "He's perfect for Ethan I think. Besides the muscles, he's just a nice guy. Ethan seems comfortable."

"I hope when we get back he's still with him," Elliot says.

"I'll make sure he doesn't mess up a good thing," Sam says, laughing.

I look down at my phone and notice the time and say, "We better get going."

Elliot looks down at his phone and says, "Shit, yeah."

We make our way to the airport and I know without a doubt what I have to do once we get parked. I feel in my pocket for the engagement ring box and smile as I take my hand out and place it on my carry on bag.

"You guys need anything before we get there?" Sam asks.

"If we forgot something we'll get it over there," Elliot says, looking back at me and smiling.

Sam parks the car close to the entrance doors and as we get out of the car, I stop Elliot and say, "I have to do something before we go in."

Elliot looks over to Sam and back at me and says, "What's up?"

I set my bags to the side and pull the box out of my pocket as I get down on one knee. I look over to Sam who instantly starts smiling and back over to Elliot who seems confused as hell as to what I'm doing.

"Elliot," I say with the box rested on my knee, "since the day I've met you, I knew that I had to have you in my life. I knew that you were something special and that you were going to change me in ways that I couldn't explain. I knew that you were sent to me for reasons I can't explain and that I was meant to get to know you."

I put the box out in front of me and display the ring as I watch Elliot's mouth drop and Sam snicker from the side.

"I know without a doubt that the only days I want to spend on this Earth are days with you in them. I want and need you in my life more than anything. I know this is a weird place to ask this, but I want to get this out before London."

I pull the ring out of the box and place it between my fingers.

"Elliot," I say, "will you proudly do me the honor of spending the rest of your life with me as husband and, well, husband?"

A tear runs down his cheek and he says, "Yes."

I put the ring on his finger and he grabs me so tightly I can't breathe as he plants a kiss on my mouth.

"I love you," I say.

"I love you, too," he says, looking at the ring on his finger.

"Wow," Sam says, leaning off the car and walking over closer to us. "Wasn't expecting this."

"Bye, Samuel," Elliot says as he hugs Sam and grabs his bags.

"Bye, bud," Sam says.

He turns to me and smiles and says, "Thank you."

"For what?"

"Making him happy. I'd want no one else to join our little circle."

He embraces me for a hug and I laugh and say, "Let me know when you want to come over and I'll get it all situated for you."

"I will," he says. "You take care of him over there."

"I will," I say.

We wave off Sam and make our way to the entrance gate and wait for our flight.

"Things are really about to change," Elliot says, looking out the window at the scattered planes.

"For the better," I say.

He looks over at me and smiles and says, "I don't even want to go now. I want to go get married and move into our house."

"It will all be there when we come back," I say.

He leans his head on my shoulder as I stare out the window and imagine everything that is waiting for us once we land in London. I think about our new apartment that's fully furnished and the traffic and the people and just how different the labels will be on the same body wash I get in America or if they'll be different at all.

I smile and realize that everything has a purpose and everything happens for reasons that we can't explain. Finding Elliot forever changed me in ways he'll never know and all I can do is think about all of the ways, as we spend our lives together, that I can remind him that he is the reason that I get up in the morning.

He is the reason that I finally feel happy and alive again. He is the reason that I no longer go to a bench late at night and wonder what life would be like if things were different. He is the reason I can breathe again without gasping for air.

66432638R00167

Made in the USA
Lexington, KY
13 August 2017